LU
STORIES

Edited by harriet c. brown

CASSAVA REPUBLIC

Abuja - London

This edition first published in 2022 by Cassava Republic Press
Abuja – London

© documenta und Museum Fridericianum gGmbH
© of the texts, of their authors and authors, 2022
© of the translations, of their translators and translators, 2022
© of this edition, Cassava Republic Press 2022

All rights reserved. No part of this book may be reproduced, stored in a retrieval system, or transported in any form or by any means (electronic, mechanical, photocopying, recording or otherwise), without the prior written permission of the publisher of this book.

The moral right of harriet c. brown to be identified as the editor of this work have been asserted by them in accordance with the Copyright, Designs and Patents Act 1988.

This is a work of fiction. Names, characters, businesses, places and incidents are either the product of the author's imagination or are used fictitiously. Any resemblance to actual persons, living or dead, events or locales is entirely coincidental.

A CIP catalogue record for this book is available from the National Library of Nigeria and British Library.

ISBN: 978-1-913175-54-2
eISBN: 978-1-913175-55-9

Designed and typeset by Deepak Sharma (Prepress Plus)
Cover & Art Direction by Leah Jacobs-Gordon

Printed and bound in Germany

Distributed in Nigeria by Yellow Danfo
Distributed worldwide by Ingram Publishers Services

www.blauer-engel.de/uz195
- resource-conserving and environmentally friendly manufacturing process
- low emission printing
- primarily made from waste paper **MA8**

Stay up to date with the latest books, special offers and exclusive content with our monthly newsletter.

Sign up on our website:
www.cassavarepublic.biz

Twitter: @cassavarepublic
Instagram: @cassavarepublicpress
Facebook: facebook.com/CassavaRepublic
Hashtag: #LumbungStories #ReadCassava

Table of Contents

Prologue — 5

Super Salve — 15
Azhari Aiyub (translated by Mikael Johani)

In the Shadow of Icarus — 51
Uxue Alberdi (translated by Jonathan Rackstraw)

Expandable Memory — 77
Cristina Judar (translated by Julia Sanches)

Dry and Green — 99
Nesrine Akram Khoury
(translated by Jonathan Wright)

The People of North Igra — 129
Yasnaya Elana (translated by Joshua Rackstraw)

Ukuza kukaNxele Or, Time Passes — 157
Panashe Chigumadzi

WTF Are Commons? — 233
Mithu Sanyal (translated by Lucy Jones)

Authors — 249

Translators — 252

Publishers — 254

Prologue

We are beings-in-common.
harriet c. brown

Every book is the work of a collective. Or rather, the process by which every book is produced is a collective project. The object you are holding in your hands takes this conviction to the extreme. Books are created by a variety of visible, recognisable individuals. There are those who write and sometimes those who translate, those who correct, who model and design, who make the cover, someone who edits and publishes it, distributes it, recommends it, sells it and, with a little luck, there are those who read it. This book, in addition to participating in that usual network, is an exercise in experiencing community. The French philosopher Jean-Luc Nancy makes a play on words that emphasises sharing and the daily experience of community: être-*en*-commun ('being-in-common'). Putting the emphasis on that *en* ('in' or 'between'), between you and me, this adventure begins.

This book, and the project that sustains it, were born in an online group chat in February 2021, during a pandemic. The team of curators behind the artistic event documenta, which takes place each five years in Kassel, Germany, got in touch with consonni, a small publisher based in Bilbao, in Northern Spain. The invitation that was sent does not resemble the enigmatic, original, and literary one described by Enrique Vila-Matas in his book *Kassel no invita a la lógica* (2014, Engl.: The Illogic of Kassel, 2015). This one is more profane, and direct. But no less exciting and irresistible. Vila-Matas says that, behind the legend of Kassel, there is the myth of the avant-garde. No less, no more!

A meeting, with many unknown faces sharing a screen. In past decades, documenta was organised by one or two people, artistic commissioners, but this time, no less than 14 people make up the Artistic Team. The Indonesian art collective ruangrupa, responsible for directing documenta in its 15th year, are focusing on the idea of the collective as a way to work together in a trustful and expansive manner. The idea of the shared expands and permeates everything. There is an Indonesian word that is repeated in all their communications: *lumbung*. A word once unknown to consonni that, like a seed or virus, grew and spread until it infiltrated the everyday vocabulary of everyone it touched. It is already part of your vocabulary. It has a particular sonority and materiality. Pronouncing it forces

the lips to arch like someone about to give a kiss.
lumbung.

lumbung is an Indonesian word referring to a rice barn that welcomes and represents community work. A collective resource based on the principle of communality. Associated with this concept is a series of values such as transparency, locality, generosity, independence, and a sense of humour: these are the tools used to create this documenta fifteen. *lumbung* is not only the theme, or a concept on which the event is structured; it is also a practice, a way of doing things, a contagious shared attitude that will bring this event to life.

In that meeting, those smiling faces, unknown yet friendly, show documenta fifteen's publication plan, which will be undertaken by the German publisher Hatje Cantz, specialised in art. One of those friendly faces, from the documenta fifteen Artistic Team, launches a question towards consonni:

'Where do you see yourselves in this programme?'

A few days later, consonni presents the idea to become artistic editor of two of the planned publications for documenta fifteen, including a concept. In the meantime, another text has caught their attention. It is an essay that aspires to locate and describe the lumbung cosmology. In other words, an expert reflecting, from an anthropological perspective, on the existence of other ways to name collective work in different parts of the world. consonni proposes to turn the book you are currently holding in your hands into a larger project, one to which many networks contribute.

consonni proposes the use of fiction and literary narratives to reach this goal. Multispecies philosopher Donna Haraway says that we need narratives that help us imagine worlds with more meaning. This is a desire shared by consonni. So, an anthology of fiction, written by authors who work with whatever word is used in their territory to talk about *collective*.

Mexican writer Cristina Rivera Garza reminds us that the writing/community duality passes through complex bridges that involve both production and distribution. consonni points out that the production of the book must also be collective. Different publishers must be involved, creating separate editions in unison, around the world. So, what was going to be an essay book with just an author exploded into a thousand pieces, and these particles multiplied and spread under the sole principle of *lumbung, tequio, auzolan...*

The Coven is born.

Crowdfunding, *forking*, and *remixing* are all words that have been created (or repurposed) to describe the process of collective work in the era of Web 2.0. However, tracing the roots of more familiar words gives us a better idea of experiences of community. Words such as *minga* in many South American countries, *tequio* in Mexico, *auzolan* in the Basque country, *andecha* in Asturias, *mutirão* in Brazil, *ubuntu* in various African countries, *gadugi* in Cherokee communities, *talkoot* in Finland, *guanxi* in China or *naffir* in Arabic are used to discuss the idea of 'being-in-common', ancestral and related. The origin, the etymological root, and the evolution of these terms (and even their current use) differs in each case, but the important thing is that they offer us a possibility; the inherited opportunity to imagine the common together. A node in the production of communality of the Mesoamerican people is the concept and practice of collective work commonly known as *tequio*: an activity that, Rivera Garza reminds us, unites nature with humanity through ties that range from creation to recreation in contexts that are radically opposed to the idea of property and to what is typical of global capitalism.

It is liberating to imagine and understand community as an everyday experience of being-in-common that has been transmitted from generation to generation, in practice and through orality and writing. Jean-Luc Nancy links this idea of community to literature. Mobilising the words to indicate the limit of human expression. More important than the content or the message is the sharing that accompanies thought, the arts, and any existence-in-common. According to Nancy, the most solitary of writers writes only for the other, and anyone who writes for him or herself, or for the anonymity of the crowd, is not a writer. Vila-Matas says: 'one writes to bind the reader, to take possession of them, to seduce, to subjugate, to enter the spirit of another and stay there, to move them, to conquer them...'. Although the transformative power of literature, in concrete and grounded cases, may be limited, thinking of writing in terms of rewriting, as an unfinished exercise, as a technique that produces that being-in-common in communality, gives meaning to this work, and guides it.

Thus begins the laborious process to locate those ancestral ways of naming collective work, to know the context and the editorial system, to locate each publisher that might have the right profile and interest in participating in the project. Independent publishers that publish fiction in different geopolitical contexts. It is also important to involve hegemonic and minority languages, so that they coexist. And to put the cultural contexts, history, and conflicts that are part of every language, into dialogue.

Inquiring into their own network, consonni contacts the Almadía publishing house in Mexico, and Txalaparta in the Basque country, to work on the concepts of *tequio* and *auzolan* - words whose use is commonplace and habitual, in their contexts. The Arab publisher Al-Mutawassit is reached after consulting and convening the network of networks. Through connections from documenta fifteen's curatorial team, Marjin Kiri from Indonesia and Cassava Republic Press from Nigeria are reached. It is an investigative process based on complicity. Dublinense from Brazil is found thanks to the International Alliance of Independent Publishers to which Txalaparta, Marjin Kiri and Dublinense belong. consonni meets, in person, with these publishers at the International Conference of Independent Publishers, organised by the Alliance in Pamplona in November 2021, where hundreds of professionals from more than 40 countries around the world gathered.

In these meetings, a declaration is made in favour of publishing which is diverse, independent, decolonialised, environmentalist, feminist, liberal, social, and solidary. It is committed to the cultural, social, and political nature of the book. Reading is presented as a liberating practice, an act of critical citizenship that takes an active and conscious part in its community. This is the spirit that permeates this book, and the program that sustains it. The independent publishers that are part of this project are, above all else, interdependent. Publishers-in-common. Vandana Shiva, as ambassador of bibliodiversity, spoke in Pamplona about the need for the micro, about the greatness of small publishers organised in vibrant networks of mutual aid. The network that has been built as a result of its production, based on cooperation, is more important than the visible book object itself.

Each publisher proposes its usual ecosystem of production and distribution. It raises those who write, those who can make use of fiction, to recreate the idea of the common in an unprecedented way. The Almadía publishing house, to write about *tequio,* presents Yàsnaya Elena Aguilar, who uses Spanish. Txalaparta presents Uxue Alberdi, who writes in Basque, to imagine around the idea of *auzolan*. Dublinense gives us Cristina Judar, writing in Portuguese about *mutirão*. Al-Mutawassit proposes Nesrine A Khoury, who writes in Arabic on *naffir*. Cassava Republic Press presents Panashe Chigumadzi, writing in English about intergenerational and transhistorical struggle through *ubuntu*. About *allmende,* Hatje Cantz and documenta fifteen have Mithu Sanyal, who uses German. And about *lumbung,* Marjin Kiri presents the writer Azhari Ayub, whose language is Indonesian. From the speculative essay and an experimental text, to the intimate story that portrays collective work as something every day and habitual, to more situated narratives. Overcoming the simplistic dichotomy between realism and fiction, words are used to produce reality rather than represent it. It is about narrating a story and placing it in the here and now, from which each person writes in the midst of constant threat of contamination. Each publishing house creates an edition in its language and distributes it in its context. Each object-book will be the same, yet different. A different cover, a different design, an altered structure, converted content. An own way of working, coordinated with the rest of the publishers. The translation required in this project, therefore, is fundamental, enormous, and demanding. We work with a group of professional translators that each publisher proposes, locates, and presents to the rest of the group. To reveal these stories through translation. Pay attention to its etymology: to translate is to go from one space to another. We moved from one community experience to another. consonni has been mediating that movement, trying to organise a balanced, yet asymmetrical, choreography.

Words mobilise what we have in common, fiction weaves networks. Fictions such as those built by religion, sport or music demonstrate their power to mobilise in the social sphere. All living organisms are based on diversity, which is why we need plurality, and diversity in our oral and written stories, to live. Collective is the process of production, reproduction, and expropriation through which this book is generated, in constant corporeal contact, under the principles of cooperation and contagion. We are beings-in-common.

Super Salve

Azhari Aiyub

Translated from Indonesian by Mikael Johani

1

What happens in this story occurred during the years of Military Operation in Aceh, when dozens of secret prison camps were set up by the Indonesian Army Special Forces, Kopassus, to torture guerilla fighters from the Free Aceh Movement. Two of the biggest prison camps were called Rancong and Rumoh Geudong. Only a handful of prisoners were able to make it out alive from the camps; one of them was Syahdi, who told the following story on the day he turned 59.

Syahdi spent time in one of the camps between July and August 1993 in Lhokseumawe, a jail complex converted from a building owned by Mobil Oil. The Kopassus christened it 'The Bat Camp' to distinguish it from another prison in the same building complex.

At The Bat Camp, Syahdi shared a cell with a dying prisoner, a tigress called Baiduri. The tigress was around 15 years old when Syahdi was brought into the cell, he recalled.

Baiduri was believed to be tigress belonging to a local shaman called Leman, who was famous for his special power to cure wounds using natural ingredients that he distilled into a copper-coloured super salve, which had a pungent smell and was initially used to treat wild animals. Later on, Kopassus soldiers kept finding the super salve in the shirt pockets of captured guerilla fighters, who swore it could cure gunshot wounds in a matter of days. When more guerilla fighters were captured with the stinky ointment in their pockets, the special forces decided to put Leman's name down on their wanted list.

The Kopassus found it difficult to capture Leman, not because he was an especially slippery enemy, but because he didn't have the one weakness that other guerilla fighters had. These were hard men, but in the end they would always surrender to the authorities once they kidnapped their children, wives, or parents. Family was their Achilles heel. But Leman lived alone in the middle of the Maja Forest. There were rumours circulating among the other forest-dwelling shamans that Leman had raised two tigers he adopted since they were cubs. Both were female. A famous shaman from Nisam even said once, 'Leman was like a mother to those tigresses.'

The Kopassus soldiers thought they might be able to capture one of the tigresses and bait Leman to come out of hiding. This tactic would only work, their commanders thought, if both these prerequisites were fulfilled:
1. They could actually capture one of Leman's tigresses.
2. Leman actually loved the tigresses like a mother.

Syahdi was not sure how long the tigress had been at The Bat Camp when he arrived there, but it must've been a while already. When he saw it for the first time in its cell, the tigress was emaciated and weak, even though he thought, given the opportunity, it would still have enough strength to knock down one or two Kopassus soldiers with a single strike of its massive paws.

If Baiduri was indeed Leman's pet tigress, and that its master had let it practically rot in a Kopassus cell, it could be that the two were actually conspiring to launch a psych-war on the government soldiers: entrapping them in bottomless doubt in their own mind. They had never received any training in taking care of a captured enemy tiger, not for any length of time. Meanwhile, Leman was safe in the knowledge that the Kopassus soldiers would not torture or rape this peculiar prisoner, monstrous tactics they never thought twice about inflicting on their human prisoners. Leman and his tigress had already won half the battle. The tigress would end up dying of old age in the care of the Kopassus by the war's end, and Leman would never have to spend time in The Bat Camp or any other prison camps. His name would never have found its way into the long list of separatists who had surrendered or been killed.

But meanwhile, the Kopassus had made their own moves to outmanoeuvre Leman and Baiduri.

Syahdi knew four other men had been taken to The Bat Camp before himself. They were Abu Neh, Idham, Farabi, and a man nicknamed The Mute. Before parting ways a few years before they met again in the camp, the men worked as loggers in the Maja Forest. Just like they did with Syahdi, the Kopassus soldiers picked up the four of them in separate places at around the same time, then brought them together to see the tigress, to help the soldiers decide if the tigress was indeed Leman's pet. Their reasoning was simple, if the tigress didn't kill the loggers instantly, then it must've been familiar with their scent, maybe even knew them well. This would make it more likely that the tigress was Leman's and fulfil the first requirement they set themselves to capture the shaman.

Unfortunately, the four loggers never stood a chance. The tiger killed them swiftly one by one; it didn't recognise any of them. Through tears Syahdi described how he saw their bones scattered all over the floor in Baiduri's cell.

The Kopassus soldiers nearly gave up with this guessing game until they kidnapped and captured Syahdi, the last logger left from the group and one that they had severely underestimated.

Syahdi had left the other loggers a long time ago, years before he was kidnapped by the Kopassus. His only remaining contact was with Farabi who earned his coins as a tough guy at the Panton Labu bus terminal. Twice a year he would deliver Leman's super salve to Syahdi. Leman never trusted anyone but Farabi to deliver his magic ointment. Syahdi had no idea how Farabi got hold of the ointment from Leman. Before he was captured by the Kopassus, he didn't even know the shaman was on their wanted list. Leman had cured him of a leg injury when he was 12 years old. His left leg had almost gone lame after a horrific accident and Leman had patiently treated it with his super salve for weeks. For years after that, Syahdi was addicted to the super salve. He could not go anywhere without it. A 500 gram tin of the salve would last around five months. The last time Syahdi bought the super salve from Leman was eight months before he was kidnapped. That meant Farabi was kidnapped and fed to the tigress not long after he delivered the ointment to Syahdi. Meanwhile, Leman must've kept making the salve at his hiding place, the location of which only Farabi knew.

Syahdi suspected that when Leman was treating his lame leg, at the same time he was also treating a tigress that was still feeding its cubs. It was only a suspicion initially, since he never actually saw any tiger in the hut where Leman lived. Maybe, for some reason or other, Leman had hidden the tiger from Syahdi. His suspicion was only confirmed much later when a tigress carcass was found inside Leman's hut.

Syahdi didn't know if Baiduri the tigress that was kept at the Bat Camp was one of the cubs whose mother Leman had cured with his super salve. But every time the Kopassus soldiers brought Syahdi to Baiduri, the tiger never once attacked him. In fact, it would lick him all over his neck, cheek, and back, leaving painful scratches from its razor-sharp tongue.

2

16 years before the loggers' kidnapping, Syahdi's uncle Latif took him to a sawmill in Maja Forest. The mill was located close to a river, hidden beneath gigantic trees. It took them nearly five hours to reach the location on foot from the

nearest village. Syahdi stayed at the mill for two years, working as a cook for five workers, before he was forced to leave because of an accident that left him with a limp on his left leg.

The mill was where Syahdi saw a tiger for the very first time. The majestic creature was walking serenely on the other side of the river after emerging from an opening in the canyon. Tigers would come to the river to drink and then return to the dark forest. Some of them would stroll aimlessly, watching the loggers struggle with lumber on the other side of the river. They would disappear behind the late afternoon fog before reappearing a few days later. At night, workers at the sawmill would hear their roars loud and close, as if they were prowling just outside the gate of the mill. The river was less than 60 metres wide and the mill was not too far from the river's edge, but it was too deep and the current too rapid for the tigers to cross.

When he first arrived at the mill, Syahdi tried to distinguish one tiger from another by the colouring on their faces, and the distinctive stripes on their foreheads and cheeks. It was hard to do so from a distance, so most of them looked identical. Except for a tigress that one day appeared with her three cubs, who were maybe around six months old. Syahdi had just finished rinsing rice in the river, one of his morning chores, when the tiger family turned up. He watched as the mother guided the cubs into the river and taught them how to swim. They came again the next day, and for the next three or four days, and every day Syahdi watched them closely. He told his uncle Latif about the tiger family when he was eating his dinner; leftover rice made slightly more palatable after being drenched in piping-hot instant noodle soup. Latif wasn't overly impressed. He said Syahdi should stop watching the tigers. Like the other four loggers, Latif never really paid much attention to the creatures. After years working at the mill, they were thankful that the mighty river provided them protection from wild animals. The only thing that worried them was the occasional raid by forest rangers trying to drive illegal loggers like them out of the jungle.

'The tigress didn't have a tail,' Syahdi said.

Idham coughed, looking displeased. He was Abu Neh's nephew and about the same age as Latif. He was like a little boss to the other workers at the mill. He had protested when Latif brought Syahdi to the site. He said children shouldn't be in the middle of the jungle, they were sure to be an annoyance sooner or later. But he couldn't do anything about it since Abu Neh, the owner of the mill, had said yes to Latif. Neh, who was 55 years old, was touched by Latif's story about his 12-year-old nephew who would surely die from being abused by his own father if they didn't save him. Latif said the boy's mother could not do anything to protect him since she had gone mad from the devil possessing her soul.

'If you don't stop watching those tigers, I'll take you back to your home tomorrow,' threatened Latif.

'Please don't, I want to stay here,' Syahdi begged.

But, intrigued by Syahdi's story, the next morning Idham walked down to the river to see the tigers for himself. He came back 15 minutes later and announced to the other workers, 'The she-devil hasn't given up.'

One by one, the workers went down to the river, only 30 metres behind the mill, following a track used to drag and drop timber into the river. As Idham said, the tigress was still there, but her cubs were nowhere to be seen. Seeing the men on the other side of the river, the tigress roared and ran agitatedly in circles. Called by their mother's mighty racket, the three cubs emerged from the river and let out their own tiny roars.

'Does she want her cubs to exact revenge on us?' Abu Neh said in a worried voice.

'Why us? We're not the ones who cut off her tail,' Farabi said. He was the biggest man out of all the loggers, with massive muscles in his biceps. He was the best axeman and the one tasked with cutting down trees.

'There was a misunderstanding,' Abu Neh said. 'But don't worry, they won't be able to cross the river. Not now, not ever.'

'I think she could,' Farabi said. 'Before Syahdi was here, I once saw it swim at least a third of the way across. It was only just beaten back by the rapids.' Farabi pointed to a spot near the middle of the river.

'Why didn't you tell us? That's very dangerous. We wouldn't have time to save ourselves,' Abu Neh said.

'You guys had gone away to the canteen that day,' Farabi said.

'I think it's time to ask for his help,' Latif said.

'You mean Leman the shaman?' Farabi said.

Latif nodded.

'He's still mad at me,' Abu Neh said.

'That's not your fault,' Farabi said. 'He thinks we're too close to the Station crew.'

'So you think we should refuse everyone who comes to the mill?' Idham said.

'You're the only one who can't wait to receive those visitors,' Farabi smirked. 'You can't live without your naked centrefolds.'

'At least I can read,' Idham said.

'I'll go and find Leman,' Latif said, ending the quarrel.

With Latif and Idham gone, the rest of the loggers worked as usual, cutting and splitting lumber into a tall pile of four-by-eight-metre flat boards wrapped in a specially knitted net. It took them at least two weeks to fill the net, which could fit at least half a cubic metre of lumber. Once they have packed ten to 12 cubic metres of flat boards, they would release them into the river. The task to supervise the process, to make sure the netted boards were carried downstream by the river current, fell to Wednesday, The Mute.

Night now came earlier. The air was cooler, but was not cold enough yet for a bonfire. Before Maghrib, Abu Neh ordered his men to board up the mill door with two thick planks of wood. They also placed three axes near the door where they could reach them easily. Farabi and Abu Neh looked nervous; so did Wednesday, though no one had bothered to explain to him what was happening. Syahdi suspected that before he came to the mill, something tragic must have happened involving the loggers and the tigress. In the morning before Latif and Idham left the mill, he heard his uncle tell Abu Neh, 'If I don't come back, take care of the kid.'

That night, the tigress let out two loud roars that shot fear into the hearts of the four loggers left at the mill, none of whom were able to go back to sleep after that. Perhaps in an attempt to suppress his fear, Abu Neh decided to tell Syahdi the story of Leman the shaman.

Abu Neh said that according to legends Leman never stayed too long at any one spot in the

Maja Forest. He was a true explorer. Every day he would walk through the forest collecting all sorts of leaves, roots, dead insects, or rare mosses. Those were the ingredients for his super salve. At first he tried it on a few people who got injured in the forest, or used it to treat wounded animals he encountered during his expeditions. But like other men and animals, Leman had his own nest on the bank of the same river, a wooden hut a three-hour walk upstream. The hut was deserted most of the time, but some pilgrims who had come to the area to meditate said they'd seen a few wounded animals in the hut that looked like they were waiting for Leman to return. The shaman had built the hut years ago as an animal clinic, and Abu Neh had helped him install the windows and the door.

It was then the dry season and Abu Neh predicted Leman was well on his way upstream, perhaps a day's walk from their mill, or even further. 'But don't worry,' he said, 'He could sniff a man from kilometres away.'

Legends said the tigers of Maja Forest worshipped Leman because he'd saved their lives many times over. According to Abu Neh, a tigress only ever teaches her cubs to swim in the presence of humans as a call to arms, since tigers don't really swim. They had to find another way, or someone else, to convince the tigress that the loggers at the mill were not her enemies.

'So who cut off her tail?' Syahdi asked Neh.

'I've no idea,' Neh replied. 'Many people live in this forest. But we've never harmed the tigers.'

'Must be people from the Station,' said Farabi, who was trying to keep himself warm inside a hammock.

'I said I didn't know. None of us know,' Neh said.

'I heard them say it myself,' Farabi said. 'They're willing to pay exorbitant prices for a tiger's tail.'

'I don't know what else I should tell you,' Neh said.

'What do you need a tiger's tail for?' Syahdi said.

'To make you invisible when you rob rich people's homes,' Farabi said.

Farabi kept interrupting Abu Neh's stories mid-sentence, unwittingly spilling the real truth that Syahdi felt everyone else was covering up. Farabi would talk over Abu Neh when he thought the older man was being less than straightforward. He didn't treat Neh with much respect at all, even though the much older man was the owner the mill. The other three loggers, on the other hand, always kowtowed to Neh. Farabi owed his brashness to his time in jail. He was barely 30, but looked much older than Latif and Idham. His parents had abandoned him at an orphanage when he was still a baby. They didn't leave any note in his cot. He grew up in the orphanage, which also doubled as an Islamic boarding school, and stayed there until one day, when he was just a little older than Syahdi, he strangled his teacher until he nearly died. He insisted during his trial that the teacher had raped him repeatedly. The judge gave him five years for attempted murder. He met Abu Neh, who was serving time for illegal logging, in his last year at the jail. When they got out, Neh recruited Farabi to be one of his loggers.

Farabi had grown close to Syahdi. He had listened to his stories about being abused by his own father and had promised Syahdi that he would teach his father a big lesson as soon as he had the chance. And one day he did just that. Before they were all kidnapped by the Kopassus, Farabi was the only logger who still kept in touch with Syahdi.

Three days later, Latif and Idham returned to the mill. They were all smiles, though absolutely knackered from their adventure.

'Did you find Leman?' Abu Neh asked them.

'We nearly did, at the Station.'

'That's a far distance from his place. He's not afraid of anything, is he?' Neh said.

'He said the tigress must've thought we were from the Station.'

'As I said, it was a misunderstanding. Is he going to tell the tigress that we're not from the Station?' Neh asked.

'He said he would try,' Latif said, 'If she walks away, that means she must've listened to him.'

'Did he accept the tobacco I packed for him?' Neh said.

Latif nodded.

Two days later the tigress and her three cubs left the river, never to be seen again. Or at least Syahdi never saw them again after he left Abu Neh's mill.

3

The accident happened seemingly out of nowhere on the day the felled timbers were due to be dropped into the river. Syahdi had supervised the process quite a few times already. The loggers needed extra assistance to do it and usually they invited young men from nearby villages to help them. The freelancers were told to cut off the rope that had kept the timbers suspended in their net above the river. The problem was that they didn't bother making sure no one was in the river. Syahdi watched as if in slow motion the timbers carried by the rapids rolling towards him. He screamed as loud as he could. The last thing he remembered was throwing himself towards the bank of the river on his right side to avoid the timber avalanche.

When he came to, he found himself in a tiny room smelling of damp and cockroach droppings. There was a single lamp made from an old margarine can. Syahdi screamed in agony from an excruciating pain in his left shin. A few moments later, someone about the same age as Abu Neh arrived. A thin, short, dark man.

'You've woken up, finally,' the stranger said. He left immediately and came back only a few hours later.

A few days later, Latif and Farabi visited Syahdi. They took turns telling him how his left leg was crushed by a piece of wood just under the knee. He was unconscious for more than a week and was now being treated at Leman's hut. When the accident happened, the loggers had almost given up trying to save his life. The nearest shaman lived a day's walk from the mill, and the nearest clinic was two days' walk away. Farabi said the only chance they had of saving his life was to bring him to Leman. Since Leman could treat wounded animals, he must have something to treat an injury to a human leg as well, Farabi reasoned. The other loggers were worried that Leman would not be home. Someone said waiting for the famous shaman to return to the hut without knowing when was tantamount to leaving Syahdi to die. But Farabi insisted Leman would be home this time around. 'If he isn't, I won't believe he could sniff other humans from kilometres away anymore.'

Without waiting for the others, Farabi lifted Syahdi to his back and started walking. 'Come with me,' he said to Latif, who looked confused. They were in luck. Leman was in his hut peeling duriàns and throwing the soft fruits into a basket when they arrived. Farabi told him what happened. Leman told them to get into the hut and lay Syahdi on a woven mat made from pandan leaves.

'You can go,' Leman said, 'Come back in a few days, same hour.'

Latif begged to stay at the hut to keep his nephew company, but Leman told him to go.

Every week Farabi and Latif took turns visiting Syahdi. They were never allowed to enter the hut. They didn't know how Leman was treating Syahdi's injured leg. He only told them that Syahdi was getting better and that they should trust in his method. Syahdi himself said Leman never massaged his injured leg, only slathering his super salve on it three times a day. Leman hardly ever spoke to him, except to give him instructions on how to treat his leg.

Syahdi didn't feel comfortable staying with Leman and begged the loggers repeatedly to take him home. Unlike at the mill, Syahdi felt incredibly lonely in Leman's hut. He could hear everything from inside his room; the mysterious whoosh of the wind, the stream in the river, the sounds of birds and insects that he never heard at the mill, the distant sound of women splitting rice in a mortar, and, when the west wind blew, the sound of an electric saw, sometimes a distant hum and more often a very loud roar. Then there were the sounds inside the hut itself; soft but very definite, somewhere between a snore and an insistent scratching, something both hard to describe but very distinctive that Syahdi still remembers to this day.

The hut only had one bedroom where Leman slept. The door was always locked. Syahdi thought the distinctive noise he heard came from inside the room. When night came and it was dead quiet, the snoring and scratching grew louder, only sometimes obscured by the screeching of monkeys on top of the hill on the other side of the river. Syahdi was convinced there was another creature living with them inside the room, but he was unsure what kind.

In his fifth week there, once the sun was up in the morning, Leman took Syahdi out to the yard to stretch his legs for 30 minutes. They did this every day until week seven, when Leman upped the dose to an hour every morning. Syahdi was too weak to walk on his own at first, but Leman patiently guided him. When Syahdi was too tired to even lift his legs, Leman told him to rest on a gazebo in the yard.

There Syahdi watched Leman collect a bunch of leaves, roots, and seeds from a row of baskets and place them in the yard to dry under the sun. Leman would then end his morning routine by cracking open a few durians and storing their soft-fleshed fruits inside another basket.

One morning, Syahdi was sitting in the gazebo to rest when he saw Leman hurry into the hut, leaving half-opened durians near the door. He came back out carrying a hunting rifle. He placed the rifle inside the durian basket and gazed at Syahdi, and then to the direction of a walking trail nearby.

'Can you go inside?' he asked Syahdi.

Syahdi shook his head. Leman swore at himself. Syahdi knew he was calculating his next moves. He grabbed Syahdi and took him inside the house.

'Stay here, don't come out,' Leman said. But he left the door open.

Syahdi watched as Leman went back to his work. Usually, it took him less than ten minutes to crack open ten durians. But this time he had 50 durians in two big baskets to split open. He struck the durians in anger with his machete. When he finished with the first basket, four men appeared on the dirt trail. They were not Abu Neh's loggers. Leman greeted them and offered them the already peeled durians. But the men didn't come for the fruits, instead they started arguing with Leman. They were about to beat him up when Leman reached for his rifle and aimed it straight at their faces. They beat a hasty retreat. Syahdi heard one of them scream out that they were going to burn down Leman's hut.

Leman stayed in the gazebo for quite some time with the rifle in his hands. He didn't know what to do. He kept looking at his hut and then at the dirt trail next to it.

'Get ready,' Leman said after a while to Syahdi, 'I'll get you back to the mill.'

'But I can't walk,' Syahdi said.

Leman swore at himself again, then said, 'I'll carry you.'

They'd only walked a few paces when Latif and Farabi appeared at the end of the dirt trail. Leman welcomed them with a few choice expletives. He was afraid they weren't going to come. Farabi said they needed to take care of a few things and time slipped by. Leman told them what happened. Farabi told him he could stay at the hut and guard them, but Leman said that was a bad idea. He said he wasn't worried by the men's threat, but he was worried about Syahdi. His condition had improved enough to return home, but he still needed to put his leg muscles to work more often if he were to recover completely.

'Okay then, we'll take him home right now,' Farabi said.

'If only he could stay a bit longer with me…,' Leman said. You could hear guilt in his voice.

'I'm sure I could cure his legs completely. But he can't stay here. I'm so sorry, but throughout his life there will be times when his leg will hurt again terribly.'

Leman went into his room and came back with a jar of his copper-coloured super salve. 'This should be enough for six months. When it runs out, come back here to pick up some more,' Leman said. He then gave them instructions on how to apply the salve.

They arrived back at the mill in the afternoon and Syahdi was elated. It felt like he had been freed from something repressive that he could not quite put his finger on. At the mill he felt like he was among friends. He didn't care that he was going to have to spend the next six months in bed.

Three days after Syahdi left, people set fire to Leman's hut. Hearing the news, Farabi immediately set out to find Leman. People warned him it would be dangerous, but he didn't care.

'I only found the charred remains of a tigress and her cub inside the hut,' Farabi said when he came back. 'The cub was still suckling on its mother.'

The workers at the mill didn't want to look at Syahdi when they heard the news. They could hear his cries of anguish. Syahdi thought about what would happen if Leman didn't act quickly to rush him out of the house. Maybe his charred remains would be found next to the tigress and the cub. He was right though, other creatures were living in that hut. Tigers. If the burned tigress was the same one he saw across the river at the mill, did she bring her three cubs with her? It was possible there were more tigers at the hut. It all happened so fast; the hut was set on fire only two days after the men threatened Leman. Did he have time to save the other two cubs? Syahdi kept all these questions to himself. Only later would he tell Farabi about them.

Syahdi told Farabi it was people from the Station that had threatened Leman and that they'd visited and stayed at the mill before.

'Edi and Edo?' Farabi asked.

Syahdi nodded.

Station people are men who worked at the big machined mill where they processed only semantok and meranti trees with diameters of at least three metres and up to four metres. People called it the Station because before it was turned into a mill, its location, the highest point in the Maja Forest, had previously housed a military radio station that was hastily erected after the government launched their first Palapa satellite. The loggers at Abu Neh's mill had only heard stories about the radio station's impressive tower, which reached as high as the top of the tallest coconut tree. It was the Station people who spread the legend. The loggers had never seen the tower for themselves since the area was immediately fenced off when the soldiers came. They could not imagine a man-made structure as high as that. The government had sent in six soldiers to guard the area. Since then they'd arrested a few trespassers, who were all charged with obstructing radio waves from the tower.

Around a year after the tower was erected, dozens of nok buffaloes were seen pulling boxes past the old sawmills scattered along the Maja River. One of the buffalo riders said they were paid a handsome sum to deliver the boxes to the Station. They received the boxes from pick-up truck drivers who had earlier unloaded them off a large truck that had struggled to get through the narrow and muddy village road. 'What's inside the boxes?' the rider said, 'They told me it's a device to sharpen the pictures on your TV screen.'

A few days later the riders drove back past the mills with only half the number of buffaloes in their possession. 'Once they saw how strong these noks were, they insisted on taking them off our hands,' one rider said.

No one back then knew who 'they' were. Three days later, along with more noks and more workers, came dozens of other people in three waves. Their uniform was odd-looking and out of place: raincoats, helms, and heavy boots, right in the middle of the dry season. They didn't say much. The loggers assumed they were sent to operate the Station.

Two weeks after the last group of people had arrived at the Station, a loud machine-like sound was heard emanating from the fenced-off area. It sounded like thunder. Loggers at the mill that was located far upstream relayed the news that they could see the top of the broadcast tower illuminated in lights at night.

Electricity had arrived. Then the loggers started to notice the dirty water in the river. Sometimes they could hardly see the water for all the logs that flowed endlessly downstream. The loggers noticed sawmarks they'd never seen before on the trunks and branches, much sharper and less rough than their own handiwork. Then came the wild animals. They started appearing on the other side of the river, including tigers. Many of them looked confused. One or two in panic tried to cross the river and were drowned by the rapids. As if things weren't bad enough, a few months later the loggers in Maja Forest were arrested in a raid targeting illegal loggers. Their mills were set on fire, the logs they felled confiscated, the workers stripped naked and beaten, and the mill owners — one of them was Abu Neh — were put on trial. He was sentenced to eight months.

Neh had been a logger for more than half his lifetime before he had to spend a night in jail. A saw was the only tool he was familiar with. That was why a year after his release he returned to the Maja Forest, to the exact same spot where he used to fell trees, on his own.

Abu Neh wasn't afraid because he had learned during his trial that small-time loggers like him were only forbidden from felling trees with a trunk diameter of more than one metre. Beyond that he had to apply for a permit like the big-time loggers at the Station. He planned to fell only small trees to avoid the law. Business was good enough that not long after he recruited two workers; one was Farabi, a friend who used to share his cell, the other Wednesday, a mute he met on a Wednesday at a bus station. Latif and Idham joined them not long after.

Abu Neh met Leman when he was cleaning up the remains of his old mill that had been burned down. He knew Leman's father, a famous shaman who had joined Daud Beureueh's Army of Islam. His son did not join the army, though. Neh had heard rumours that Leman had won a few duels against tigers which he did for fun. Leman was a small svelte man with a dark complexion. There were scars all over his roundish face, They looked like scars from tiger's claws. When he met him, Leman looked younger than Abu Neh, who was 46.

Leman had offered a job to Abu Neh to build a hut near a cliff deep in the forest. He was going to use the hut to treat wounded tigers. He said the Station was going to be here for quite some time.

'They're building a liquid gas power plant in the north. Almost as big as this forest. The government will need even more wood,' Leman told Neh. He seemed to know a lot about what was happening at the Station and the world outside Maja Forest.

Abu Neh knew the Station was here to stay, but he had no idea about the liquid gas plant. The furthest he had gone from his old mill was to the jail in the district capital. The north Leman mentioned was located in another district. He thought it was odd that someone with a reputation as a tiger killer now said he wanted to build a clinic to treat wounded tigers. But he didn't want to pry. His new mill was only starting out, so he took on the job to build Leman's hut.

Once his mill was running again, quickly followed by other mills (though not as many as before the government started rounding up illegal loggers), workers from the Station sometimes would come and stay, especially during the wet season. The constant rain made the track to the Station almost impenetrable. They had to move so slowly that often they were forced to stay a night or two at Neh's mill. They never came empty handed. They would be on their way back from doing their monthly shopping in the city and picking up mail and packages from the post office. They would share packs of white cigarettes, ground coffee, instant noodles, canned foods, milk, batteries, and even cards with pictures of naked white women on the back, with the loggers at Neh's mill. They would share the latest rumours they heard in the city and, one time, even offered a job to hunt wild animals for their organs. They continued to visit Neh's mill when Syahdi was living there. He saw them a few times, though Latif, the most religious of all the loggers, always tried to prevent his nephew from talking to them — men who on cold nights sought protection through endless bottles of liqueur and dirty stories.

When Syahdi was still recovering from his leg injury, a Station man even offered to take him to the hospital. Latif politely refused.

4

A prisoner was brought in and plonked on a chair next to Syahdi. A blinding flashlight shone right in his face. He wanted to shield his eyes with his hands but they were cuffed.

'Do you know him?' an officer asked.

The prisoner took a few seconds before answering, 'He's Syahdi, Sir.'

'Where did you know him from?'

'Maja Forest, Sir.'
'Does he walk with a limp?'
'Yes, he does, Sir.'

The officer shone the flashlight in the prisoner's face.

Syahdi adjusted his eyes to look at the prisoner's face. It was swollen all over. The skin was smashed like an overripe jackfruit. The officers must've just finished beating him up.

'Syahdi, do you know this guy?'
'No, Sir.'
'I will kill your mother if you tell me you don't know this guy's name.'

Syahdi didn't say anything. Of course they would do that. But he had no idea who the man was.

'Look at him one more time,' the officer said. 'Look closely.'

Syahdi did as he was told. He looked closely at the man's face and tried to match it with the faces of all the men he had ever known in his life, but still he could not recognize him. His banged up face made it even harder to see what he really looked like.

'I don't know him, Sir.'
'Get him out of here!'

Five minutes later. The flashlight again in Syahdi's face.

'Who is he?' the officer asked the new prisoner that was just brought in.

'Syahdi.'
'What does he do?'
'He's a logger.'
'When did you first see him working as a logger?'
No answer.
'When?'
'Maybe 15 years ago.'
'Where did you see him cutting up trees?'
'In the Maja Forest.'
'The Maja Forest is massive. Which spot?'
'Next to a river.'
'How old was he then?'
'12 I believe.'
'What were you doing in the Maja Forest?'
'I went there to meditate, Sir.'
'Meditate?'
'It was to get a magic power to get rich, Sir.'
'What business did you have with Syahdi?'
'I met him when I was staying the night over at Abu Neh's mill.'
'Did he have a limp?'
'No, Sir.'
'Flashlight.'
'Yes, Sir!' another officer answered.
'Show him his leg!'
'Yes, Sir!'
'You lied,' the main officer said, 'Look at his lame leg.'

'I didn't know, Sir! When I met him, he wasn't limping. But I swear he's the Syahdi I used to know.'

'Syahdi!'

'Yes, Sir.'

'Do you know this guy?'

Under the flashlight was a man around 60, with thick lips and a large mole on his left cheek. His face was clean; he had not been beaten like the other prisoner. Syahdi tried to remember if he was one of the visitors at Abu Neh's mill.

'No, Sir. I've never seen him before,'

'Get him out of here,' the officer said. 'How many more out there?'

'Only one left, Sir,' the junior officer said.

When Syahdi saw the last prisoner's face under the flashlight, he started crying. The man's face had been beaten into a bloody pulp. He sat motionless in his chair.

'Syahdi?'

At first Syahdi didn't say anything. He was angry. 'Fuck you,' he then said suddenly, surprising himself.

The officer noticed the change in Syahdi's demeanour. It was exactly what he was waiting for.

'Syahdi, you have two options. I'll throw your mother into the tigress's den or you answer my questions.'

'What the fuck do you want to know,' Syahdi said angrily.

'Who is this man?'
'Amir Siregar.'
'Where does he live?'
'At the Simpang Binu Store.'
'What does he do?'
'He services radios.'
'Have you known him for long?'
'About a year.'
'How did you know him?'
Syahdi did not answer.
'Syahdi... how did you know him?'
'I bought a cassette player from him.'
'Get him out of here. Enough for today.'

As soon as he arrived at the Bat Camp, Syahdi was forced to see other prisoners almost every day. They came from other prison camps the Kopassus had in the area. Syahdi saw dozens of them. The interrogators grilled them, trying to fish out information if they knew Syahdi as a logger at Abu Neh's mill. Every one of them claimed they knew him well, before and after his accident. Some of them described precisely what Syahdi did at the mill, taking care of the loggers and cooking their meals, and that he was Latif's nephew.

The officers were frustrated by Syahdi's insistence that he never saw any of the prisoners, until that day Amir Siregar was brought into his cell. Amir did not spend time in the Maja Forest 16 years ago. He'd only lived in Aceh for five years. He was brought to the interrogation as someone that Syahdi knew quite well but had no relations with the Maja Forest loggers. He was there to convince the interrogators that Syahdi wasn't lying to them by pretending he did not recognize the other prisoners. Syahdi said there were three other prisoners like Amir who were brought to see him.

Syahdi thought the prisoners who 'knew him when he lived in the Maja Forest' must have visited or stayed at Abu Neh's mill for many different reasons, including to learn the magic power to become rich. But he simply could not remember their faces. Even the mole on one of the prisoners' faces failed to jog his memory.

Now convinced that Syahdi wasn't lying, the Kopassus soldiers brought Syahdi to see two other prisoners who seemed to have a special connection with the tigress and also Leman. They had been tortured, not for the first time, before they were brought in to the Bat Camp.

They were two of the four men who made threats to burn down Leman's hut. Syahdi recognised them. They were twins and both stayed overnight a few times at Abu Neh's mill, both before and after his accident. Syahdi had observed them with wonder, since they were identical twins and Syahdi had never seen their kind. They were Edi and Edo. Edi, the older, was a supervisor at the Station and the one whose offer to take Syahdi to hospital Latif refused. They were the Station people who Farabi accused of cutting off the tail of the tigress that Syahdi saw on the other side of the river. Syahdi also knew they were the ones who tried to persuade Idham and Wednesday the Mute to hunt for tiger organs. They were prepared to pay big money for those.

15 minutes before Edi and Edo were brought to the Bat Camp, the building was shaken by the roars and cries emanating out of Baiduri the tigress's cell. Syahdi said this had never happened before. The tigress never even reacted to the smell of human's blood, even after she was left without food for days.

During their interrogation, Edi and Edo were also asked if they recognised Syahdi. Unlike the other prisoners, both of them said they didn't. No way, Syahdi thought, they must've known it was him.

When the tigress in the next cell ran amok, Syahdi heard the officers repeatedly threatening to leave Edi and Edo at her mercy if they kept refusing to tell them where Leman was hiding. One of the officers told the twins the tigress would be grateful to them for allowing her to take revenge for her mother's death 16 years ago. But Edi and Edo swore they didn't know where Leman was hiding. Syahdi thought the questions the officers asked the twins seemed to suggest both of them were especially close to Leman. The Kopassus soldiers accused them of distributing

Leman's salve to the guerilla fighters. Did they re-establish contact with Leman after he left the mill? Not impossible, Syahdi thought. And now they were risking their lives trying to protect Leman who was once their enemy. One thing they couldn't do anything about was the fact that their presence at the Bat Camp had raised the tigress's ire. She even started running amok when they were still outside the jail!

When Edi and Edo were brought before Syahdi, the Kopassus officers only had one question: did he know them?

Syahdi saw this was his chance, a chance as tiny as the space between the teeth of a saw and a tree trunk it was cutting into, which the officers unwittingly provided to weigh up his answer carefully. His first thought was to protect Leman. That must be what the other four loggers had done before him. If he told the officers that he knew Edi and Edo, he knew they would not be able to withstand Baiduri's wrath and would tell them where Leman was as soon as they had the chance. Syahdi also knew that whatever his answer was, he was bound to meet the tigress sooner or later.

'Syahdi?' the officer said, 'Do you recognise these bastards?'

'No,' Syahdi said, 'I've never met them before in my life.'

Banda Aceh, 16 January 2022

Notes

Military Operation Area (DOM) was a status given by the Indonesian government to its westernmost province of Aceh in 1990-1998. Throughout DOM, the New Order regime ran the Red Net Operation, a military operation combining warfare and intelligence designed to crush the Free Aceh Movement separatist group. During this counter-insurgency operation — run by the Kopassus, Indonesian Army's Special Forces — there were multiple allegations of human rights abuses committed by Indonesian soldiers.

The Free Aceh Movement (GAM) was a separatist group led by Hasan Tiro that was founded in 1976 with the intention to free Aceh from the Unitary Republic of Indonesia. The group survived for 30 years before signing a peace accord with the government of Indonesia in Helsinki, Finland in 2005.

Mobil Oil is a multinational corporation founded by Exxon and Indonesian government-owned Pertamina to exploit the gas and oil reserves in Arun, North Aceh. During the DOM in Aceh, ExxonMobil was allegedly aiding and abetting the Indonesian military to commit human rights abuses.

In The Shadow of Icarus

Uxue Alberdi

*Translated from Basque and Spanish
by Joshua Rackstraw*

> *prior of flowering, the epoch of mastery
> before the appearance of the gift,
> before possession.*
>
> The Doorway, Louise Glück

1

We are tense, backed into a corner by our adolescence. We compare the heights of our friend's balconies to see if they are high enough for the fall to be fatal. Oihana and Lore live on the seventh floor, Eli on the eighth. The blocks in our neighbourhood don't look like the houses we drew when we were kids: they are expressionless brick monsters on the side of the motorway. Now and again, we hear screeching brakes, or sudden acceleration, but the sound of the cars is usually a low, monotonous, rumble. In Eli's kitchen, her mum says: 'Eat some fruit,' as she approaches the fridge. Eli tends to gain weight easily. 'How many *faltas*?', as she revises her schoolwork. At the *ikastola*, they call mistakes *faltas*. 'Stand up straight!' They make us do dictation even in summer. We are defined by our shame. Lore has her wet hair tied up in a tight bun; she's doing kick ups with the ball, she doesn't trust our childish femininity. Oihana buys tobacco for her mother from the store on the corner.

The house belongs to our father in the afternoons: he works, and we keep quiet. I see him, hunched over his papers. We are cultured. We have a world map in the bathroom, constellations on the ceiling, books on the shelves, a globe in the bedroom. *Aita* strikes a match when he has a bowel movement. As an exercise in humility, he makes me write the letter *t* over and over again: 'You're crossing it too high.' When he's in a good mood, he comes out with random phrases in Italian: *bisogna insistere, la tua mamma, la mala testa*. My mother comes home just as they're putting on the nine o'clock news. After closing the shop, she drinks wine with her sister; they have two, sometimes three glasses, and it gets late. She also comes in late at lunch time: she jogs in her spare time. Compared to *Ama*, I lack energy. I wait, curled up on the balcony, with my bathrobe on. I've already had a shower. I breathe in the cold. I sit up when I see her coming up the hill. On the radio, we hear of the war in Yugoslavia. At home, the war comes at dinner time, before *Ama*. We eat bread without salt, we don't separate the recycling, we do sit-ups in the kitchen.

Summer crushes us against the cement as the sun lightens the hair on our thighs. We practice, every day, a type of joy, as if there is a debt to be settled. But it's getting more and more difficult. We are too big to depend on our parents, but we are not free to live our own lives. We're not in want of anything specific, but we don't know what to do with our time. I lie down in the coolness of the doorway, under the weight of 40 houses, invigorated by the smell of bleach. 'Boredom is important,' my mother tells me as she, once again, goes out.

I wait for my friends on a green bench just outside my house because I don't want *Aita* to have a go at them for not speaking Basque properly. Grammar is a hill he is willing to die on, he is fully committed to correct language use, he feels safe within the status quo. He taught me to protect myself with language. I am 11 years old, and I am moved by the verse *'when dancing, I span without touching the ground.'*[1] I speak two dialects, proper Basque at home and

---

1 Translation of a verse from the song *Nere sentimendua* ('My feeling'), by Antonio Urbieta.

Euskañol when I'm out; I have learned to hold my tongue when necessary to avoid embarrassing myself. I hear the name Induráin, called from the neighbourhood kitchens, among cheers of encouragement: he's pulled ahead of the pack, and he's in the lead. Eli walks over with a large plastic sheet under her arm. Asier has also come down. His mother throws a sandwich to him from the balcony: 'Eat the bread!' He's had a growth spurt and his body seems two sizes too big, it looks like his head has shrunk. His elbows are scratched and his legs look like wooden fence posts. He shakes a cloth bag: 'Pegs'. I open my backpack: ropes, cords and string, a hammer.

To get to Lore and Oihana's place, you have to cross the bridge over the A8. We goad truckers into honking their horns, and we don't give up until they do. At the crossroads, we sink our feet into freshly laid cement: the act of creating a permanent imprint of the soles of our shoes produces a fleeting sense of calm. On the other side of the bridge, we see blue and grey overalls hanging out to dry in the sun, puffed up by the wind. We read the graffiti on the side of the motorway, *GORA ETA, LEITZARAN EZ!, INTSUMISIOA*[2], but we do not read it out loud.

---

2 Graffiti common in the 1980s, meaning *LONG LIVE ETA, SAY NO TO LEITZARAN! REBELLION*. ETA was the paramilitary arm of the Basque independence movement, and Leitzaran was the name used to refer to a proposed

Oihana and Lore's mother invites us in over the intercom. The lift door is heavy. Inside, someone has burned the buttons with a lighter. Fragrances of *Mimosín* fabric softener and cigarette smoke escape from under the door of the house. I come here sometimes to watch TV, I'm always welcome. Karmen opens the door and greets us both with many kisses. As usual, she hugs me, and grabs my bum: 'Cute bum!' She's wearing a tracksuit and has a perm. My mum says: 'She doesn't leave the house,' and when she says it, her nostrils flare suspiciously; 'She's not well!' But I've only seen her sad once, when we were watching *Wheel of Fortune*. It was just the two of us, because Oihana and Lore were fighting in their room. She suddenly broke out in tears: she had broken her glasses. She cried for a good while, I sat silently. Today she is happy. In the living room, Lore is talking to her dad about Zülle, Rominger and Ullrich. Lore will never have hips. Kaiet appears with two large plywood boards, his chest puffed out. He's wearing fake Adidas jogging bottoms, with the three stripes glued onto the fabric. He's five years older than his twin sisters, and says he's going to help us carry the wood to the camp. Karmen gives us sweets, marshmallows and Mini Milks, bags of

---

motorway through the Leitz valley which they were opposed to, and eventually, managed to reroute.

crisps. She sends us off with a pat on the bum: 'Go on, have fun!'

On the way to San Roke, before reaching the hermitage, we turn right down a path. That's where our base is. We've spent the last few afternoons levelling the ground, nailing up pallets. Here, people take the train to the beach at Deba; we are not allowed that far from home yet. We take off our backpacks and send Asier to the fountain to fill the canteens. Once he's back, we tighten the canvas and nail the wood to the pallets that will serve as walls. Kaiet cut them to size with a saw, and with a ciggie in his mouth. Oihana came up with the design; Lore corrected it; they argued, and nobody else dared to interfere. They are smarter and more opaque than we are, for some reason. Eli and I came up with some ideas for the inside. Asier is struggling with the roof, which is the most important part; we need it to stay dry in here. We've made a sofa by putting two long pillows across three seats, which are missing their legs.

We take a break, and sit down. Kaiet pulls out some beers, challenging us with his seniority. Oihana is the only one who takes a beer, laughing for no reason. 'You're retarded,' Lore insults her siblings, kicking at a log. She works on the roof in silence, Asier helps her.

We talk about the people at the *ikastola*. Ane González's older sister has told her that she is going to put her on a diet before she gets her period. Maitane always has sweaty hands. Amaia Eguren's nipples are the colour of Strawberry Cream Chupa Chups, making you want to suck them. Jon Korta's dad beats him up; he stabbed him in the hand with a fork once. Andoni gets boners in class. We bitch about our teachers. Joxe is a perve, Xabi's a bender. The dance teacher's an alcoholic. Gorka López got told off for insulting Xabi at recess: 'Salam marikum! Salam marikum!', sticking his lips out. *Andereño* Lourdes has a tapeworm preserved in formaldehyde in the laboratory. Mirari has horse teeth, she sounds like a giant when she talks. Then the conversation drifts, we talk about our own bodies. Eli comments that her hips have widened. Oihana confesses that her boobs hurt. I've been told that I'm like an ironing board. I didn't like that one bit. It is true that my chest hasn't grown much yet. I'm not filling out. My vulva has changed, though. It smells differently to me; like lemon, like iodine. I can smell it even now, coming through my pants. I smell it all the time. I don't know if the others do too.

Kaiet opens another beer. Oihana takes out the Mini Milks, unwraps one, and tells us, 'This is how you give a blow job,' first rubbing the ice cream on the tip of her tongue, then shoving the whole thing into her mouth. I laugh, but I take the ropes and go over to Lore and Asier. I notice that Kaiet has his right hand in the pocket of his tracksuit: they say some guys masturbate like this. He takes out the lighter and lights a cigarette.

The fog is rolling in from Durango. We spread the plastic sheets over the roof, laying sticks and palm leaves on top, tying them on. The palms are also made of plastic, from an artificial plant that someone threw away. We stole the bales of straw from the *goitibehera* race. We spread the dry grass over the branches and place some flat stones on top to hold it all down. The roof seems sturdy. We check that the walls can hold it all up, and take a few steps back to admire our work. 'We should have a sleep over here,' we say.

'Shall we go in?' Oihana proposes.

We all squeeze in together, just about fitting in. It's time for our picnic. There is a scent of sugar, oil and sweat. Through the cracks between the pallets, golden dust slips in and floats in the air. Asier takes the radio cassette out of his backpack. *Sans* batteries. Dumbass. He didn't realise that there'd be nowhere to plug it in here. Even so, we set it down next to the sofa, it looks right. Eli mimes turning it on and begins to sing: 'If you wanna be my lover!' The others cheer her on, waving their heads and arms, 'I wanna ha! I wanna ha!' Our cheap bracelets jangle.

Kaiet stands at a certain distance from this childish revelry. He arches his back and looks at me with his dark eyes, the colour of shoe polish. He wrings his hands to remove shreds of tobacco. His hands are large, with rough skin. I feel as though I am being pulled by two strings: the warm breath of the group and an individual call, different, that is suddenly intimate. I join the pulse of the group, still feeling Kaiet's eyes on me.

We hear the rude sound of a drop. We look up. 'Shhh,' Lore says. Another drop. 'Storm,' she warns. We sing louder. We feel cool air coming in. At the first lick of thunder, Oihana and I tense our thighs, and squeal; we've learned that fear is sexy. Asier rubs his hands together. The three siblings put their arms around each other's shoulders. Eli shoves a handful of jellybeans into her mouth. When the downpour comes, it is euphoric. For a short time, we are free from everything we don't understand.

2

They've finished the sculpture of Icarus on the King Kong bridge. The towns around here try to rid themselves of the burden of their troubled past by commissioning works of art and olive trees to decorate plazas, bridges and roundabouts. Covering up the dirt. The figure of Icarus is made of bronze and aluminium, and hangs over the River Deba, clinging to the bridge. It is a message to the people of the town, told through the myth of the man who flew too close to the sun: this might not be the best place in the world, but don't get any big ideas, high-flyers will have their wings clipped.

I came to see the statue with my aunt. Since I started secondary school I have no place in the group of girls at the *ikastola*; it's been a few weeks since they last included me in their plans. The neighbourhood gang broke up last summer. I trust more in my future than in my present. My aunt, facing away from the statue, points to the shop, to the back window, over the river: 'That's where the water came in.' Our family disaster is the flood that snatched the business from my parents on two occasions, first in 1983, then again in 1988. Thanks to their people, they managed to scrub out the mud; remove the debris; clean up the furniture; and salvage what they could of the reels of cotton, vinyl records, and books. 'We unwound the reels until the clean thread began. If you could save a metre of thread, well, you did.'

I wish I could say that I feel that urge to make things right. To fix things with my mates, mend the broken relationship, and start over again. But I don't know how it is possible to collaborate with a group that harms you, overwhelms you, whose dynamic is lamentable. There are people who find companionship as natural as breathing; I am not one of them. 'You never know what the future holds,' says my aunt, as if reading my thoughts. I put my hands to my throat; someone has grabbed me by the hood of my sweater, almost throwing me to the ground. 'You coming?' It's Jennyfer, the school tomboy. I had already noticed her looking at me. She's with her mates. She pulls me over by the neck.

'We're going to break Marlon out,' a tall girl, with a tribal tattoo on her left arm and a hole in her lip, says. Then, by way of introduction: 'Saioa,' saluting me with two fingers to her forehead. 'He lives next to the old soccer field,' she clarifies. I understand she means Marlon. I see my aunt heading over the bridge to the shop.

Jennyfer, eating pickled onions from a transparent bag, puts her arm around my shoulders, enveloping me in the scent of sweat and vinegar. 'Do you know who he is?' she asks. I sit down. Marlon, Olegario, Fonda, Maca, Colomo. Each name tells a story. Olegario threw a butane cylinder off a fifth-floor balcony. He is also known in the village for trying to buy beer with the orange chips from the bumper cars. Fonda screwed up; he was an A* student at college, but he got kicked out of uni because of amphetamines. Or because he was too smart. Or both. He's published two books in a language of his own invention. Maca worked as a prostitute in Madrid, hears voices. She stuck a sign up on her balcony: 'House for sale. Includes husband.' Colomo learned the phone book off by heart and when you least expect it, he sings your phone number.

Going mental is a fear that has haunted me since childhood. I know it could happen. I think about what type of madness lives inside me. I know that I am more similar to Fonda and Colomo than Olegario or Maca, for example. Marlon is the most different to me because he was born like that. His nickname, Marlon Brando, was given to him ironically because he's lame, and gangly: one leg is eight inches shorter than the other, and he wears a thick heel to make up for the difference, bouncing his hips and dragging his right foot when he walks. He's always dressed in flared black trousers that hide the ugly shoe. He looks like the jack of clubs, with a blonde mane that reaches down to his chin.

'His mother has him tied up,' Saioa tells me, offended. I had heard this before. My aunt told me that he was hidden away at home until he was 18, that no one in town knew about 'that little boy that God left half-made.' Saioa adds: 'Tied up, like a dog,' and takes a right at the roundabout, where the council has planted an olive tree. We pass the nightclub, the sawmill, the petrol station. 'When he grew up and became a man, he would break out of the house to chase girls, with that limp, and his hip, and his crooked little smile,' my aunt explained. Saioa kicks a plastic bottle: 'Why would you even have kids?' I see him on Saturdays walking up the street, emitting a kind of coo, like a pigeon. He doesn't talk, he doesn't know how. Sometimes young men get him drunk; I have seen them laughing at him, making fun of his rocking gait. When he gets drunk, he calls out his name: 'Marlon-Marlon!' When we get to the cereal factory, Saioa concludes: 'They only let him out at the weekend. The rest of the time, they have a chain round his ankle.'

We leave the town, and pass the abandoned pavilions with their broken windows. The boys throw stones and bottles inside. We are a small group, five girls and two boys. We pass the graffiti, the faded posters and the 'For Rent' ads, cars with 'Wash Me' graffiti, the fibreglass ceilings. We sit on the back stairs of the *Los Herminios* bar. Nobody asks me my name; they welcome me with the smoke of their cigarettes.

Saioa takes a pair of pliers and a spray-can out of her backpack. 'I'm going in alone,' she says. The two boys decide to climb the trees in front of the house to keep an eye out for people. 'Are you gonna do the graffiti?' Saioa asks Jennyfer, who's kicking a rusty can, passing it from one foot to the other.

'What are we going to write?' she replies. They switch from Basque to Spanish constantly.

'*Marlon askatu*, right?' suggests the haggard boy who was previously mute.

'Isn't Marlon his nickname, though?' asks the girl next to Jennyfer, who is drinking a coke. No one knows Marlon's real name.

'I dunno, just put *Independentzia*' says the guy with droopy eyelids. Jennyfer dribbles the rusty can past the boy, who fails to tackle her.

'I'll figure something out,' she says.

Without thinking, I reply, 'I'll go with you.'

The house is hidden away, past the working-class neighbourhood that borders the train tracks, but before the old football pitch. Saioa explains that there's a small garden that overlooks the river, surrounded by a fence, a place where cats and ducks give birth to their incompatible litters. I'm told that Marlon is usually tied to a fence post, and feeds bread to the animals. I guess that's where he got the cooing from.

'Does he sleep out here?!' I ask.

'If you can believe it.'

We wait for the streetlamps to come on. The boys climb the trees on the other side of the road. 'Chris, give us a cig,' Saioa asks from below, and he throws the pack at her from the stumpy branch he's sitting on.

'What if he follows us?' asks the girl whose name I don't know.

'You buy him a coke, stupid,' Jennyfer replies. She points at me: 'Put your hood up.'

We take the spray can and move over to the wall of the house. It is dark, the lights are on the other side of the road. 'If I spell it wrong, tell me,' she says, looking at me as she shakes the can. I hear a 'Pssst!' from Saioa, from her hiding place in the hydrangeas, pointing to a small gap between the fence and the wall. I look across the road. I hear a car coming towards us, fast. The driver doesn't see us. I look at Jennyfer, urgently: 'Come on!'

Saioa climbs the cement wall where it joins the fence, and jumps down, quickly. She stands at the edge of the garden, her pliers in her jacket pocket, her eyes adjusting to the darkness. We've spotted Marlon, reclining on something that could be a hammock, possibly asleep. I can just make out his head, tilted to the side. I get the feeling that there are scraps of food, tins and bottles around him. A cat licks at the rubbish. It smells of urine and flowers. 'Is that where he goes to the bathroom?!' I ask Jennyfer. She puts her finger to her lips, alert. Saioa approaches slowly. I take Jennyfer's hand and, although she looks at me in astonishment, she squeezes it with hers. We catch a glimpse of two cigarette butts on the stump of the tree. Saioa is already next to the hammock. What if Marlon makes a run for it? His parents might have a gun.

The cat runs away as soon as it notices Saioa. Straining our eyes, we try to make out where the chain is attached to the wall, but it's hard to see anything clearly from our hiding place. We can't understand why Saioa is standing motionless in front of Marlon, why she doesn't crouch down to remove the chain. Is she afraid of making noise? She backs off, and steps on a bottle. We tense up, ready to escape. But nobody moves.

Saioa comes back, and neatly jumps the fence. 'It's not him,' she says. We walk in silence around the house, and stop in front of the living room window: Marlon and his mother, hand in hand, are watching TV, coloured lights reflecting on their faces. On the wall of the house, it says *Askatasuna* in red letters.

3

Jennyfer and Saioa get held back a year at school. Now we are in the same year. Saioa has very thin arms and thighs, and porn star boobs. Jennyfer has footballer legs, she looks like she rides horses. We meet in her dad's garage, who brings us metal and wood from his workshop to build a *goitibehera*. We want to make a *goitibehera* for the race on *el dia de San Juan Bosco*. We don't let the boys in, not even Jonás or Chris, Jennyfer's and Saioa's boyfriends. They go to the *gaztetxe* together, where they masturbate and smoke joints. Saioa even has sex. She calls it 'shagging'. Their tracksuits are covered in stains and holes.

They also smoke, relentlessly, when we're in the garage together. 'Roll me a joint,' they're always saying to each other. A new language opens up before me, speaking to me of violence and belonging, which I am so desperate for that it hurts. I speak to them in my fancy Basque, which, to my surprise, they love. 'You talk cool,' Saioa tells me. They want something from me, too. They usually smoke *doski*, brownish and grainy, until someone brings them a *huevo*, smuggled in their ass. When you melt the hash from the *huevo*, it bubbles up and makes your fingers sticky. I watch them, mesmerised by the movement of their fingers, their tongues, their palms. The smoke makes me dizzy; it helps me relax, gives me a break from everything that holds me down. Sitting on the floor, I check my notes for my next exam.

We take turns with the drill, the saw, and the sander. Michel, Jenny's brother, showed us how to put the *goitibehera* together. He's a junior technician at a workshop where they do sheet metal and paint. He taught Saioa how to weld while staring at her tits. We drill the tube that has the bearings attached, and insert an iron pole which is attached to the base, so that it tilts in the centre.

When we get tired, we go up to Jenny's house. It's on the fourth floor, and it smells like dog. Jenny plays music by Eros Ramazzotti, we drink

Sunny Delight and eat chips. Jenny drinks from the bottle, slaps herself on the chest, burps. Realising that I am better fed than her is a revelation for me, I reflect on the effect this has on us, on our futures. Her mother leaves notes for her on the kitchen table: 'Jenifer, I have gon to the dentest,' 'Jenny, I am at aurobics,' 'I lef you a hamburger in the frige'. I don't know how to explain the love that lies under the layers of misspellings, sugar, and saturated fats. Jenny's mother has braided hair, and writes her daughter's name differently every day.

My friends take off their enormous leather boots and lie on the sofa, stretching their legs out and smoking. 'Poisoning ourselves together is class solidarity,' says Saioa, in her torn stockings, held together with black nail polish. After a while, she says, 'Don't make a big thing out of it okay? But, I'm pregnant.'

Jennyfer stares at her, trying to find the words: 'Are you insane?' While I am not totally struck dumb, I know that I can't add anything to the conversation.

'Calm down, yeah?', she tries to reassure us. Her dad's taking her to have an abortion.

'Are you okay?' I ask. She says she is. They did it without a condom, a month and a half ago.

'Fuck am *I* supposed to do?' she says, neatly summarising the situation. I think of my father, sending a shiver down my spine. I think of my body, immaculate, imagining my ovaries to be fluffy and pink.

'If you want, we'll go with you,' I offer. She kisses me on the cheek. She smells like shampoo and smoke. They will do the abortion in Bilbao, the day after San Juan Bosco.

We go back to the garage. We tie a rope to the tube at the front to steer. We fix the V-shaped structure together with screws, and add two short boards that will act as a seat. We fit steel tubes to the sides as handles. We are not going to decorate the *goitibehera*; although there's a prize for the most originally decorated kart, we are not interested in it. We have a plan: Jennyfer will drive, I'll be in the middle, and Saioa will push us off.

Ever since I started going out with them, nobody dares mess with me. At school, we sit together, the teachers don't understand it. Jennyfer comes up behind me in the hallway, knees me in the back of the legs, then catches me before I fall, wrestles with me, plants her lips on my jugular, grabs my T-shirt collar, and pushes me up against the wall: 'You're so tiny!' Saioa puts her arm around me when she sees the girls who told me not to hang out with them. 'I'll kick your head in,' she threatened a boy she caught insulting me. Jenny grabbed the ball out from under his arm and made it dance around her feet for ten minutes, with him failing to intercept.

Wanting to give them something back, I showed them my father's library. Collections of literature, grammar books, philosophy, dictionaries, encyclopaedias: 'You can take whatever you want.' Saioa looks around, taking it all in, as though dealing with a maths problem.

Jenny says that if we added a wheel on the back, like the ones they have on supermarket trolleys, we could brake, and avoid spinning out on the corners. Some of the engineering students have installed hydraulics on their kart, but we consider that too much. Jenny insists that we find a braking system, or a handbrake at least. 'Chill,' says Saioa, who doesn't want to hear a peep about braking, 'I got this.' She is so confident that no one dares contradict her; the way she launches herself into the future sweeps anyone out of the way. 'We gonna do this or what?'

The hill in our neighbourhood is very steep. I go up it almost every afternoon, except if Jennyfer has training: she plays for the *Euskadi* regional team. I've been helping her with her homework for a few months now. She's not got the basics down in maths, or English, or Basque: it's like stoking a fire that's about to go out. She spends most of her time at school in the hall, texting Jonás. She thinks she's dumb, the teachers treat her like she's dumb. She tries to hide the pain that this causes her. She treats me roughly and passionately. She butts her forehead against mine, and kisses me hard on the lips: 'I don't get it.' I repeat the explanation. I know she can learn. She tells me that if she passes her exams, she'll snog me. I work out how far back I have to go to explain each concept to her, back to last year, back to first year. She's close to giving up: 'I'm an idiot.'

'We'll continue later.' I give her a break, 'Shall we lie down?' I massage her legs with a menthol gel. She stretches out, on her back, resting her head in her hands, the TV remote on her chest. She takes off her tracksuit for me to give her the massage. Her muscles are sore after training. She has tanned legs and very tough hair, like artificial grass on a soccer field. I run my hands up her thighs. 'Don't get too excited,' she stops me.

Sometimes she tells me, 'Come,' and takes me to bed. We lie under the flannel sheets with our bodies awake. She orders me around like this because she is embarrassed to say what she wants. On the wall there is a faded photo of Jonás, which she kisses every night before bed. It seems like a souvenir from another life, totally unrelated to us. Jenny pulls up her shirt and I stroke her back, under her sports bra, feeling her moles, her soft hair, the elastic of her knickers. She strokes me back; my waist and my back, and at the very most, the sides of my body. When I get home at sunset, I pull my shorts off quickly.

A month ago, while my father was taking a nap, I left the house and went down to the river as though marching to war, my 50 kilos at the mercy of fate. Icarus's body hung from the bridge, wings spread, cursing his hubris. She opened the door, and said 'What do you want?'

I answered, 'I'm in love with you.'

She turned her back on me. 'Yeah? I'm with Jonas.' And then: 'Come on, give us a massage.'

We have gotten the *goitibehera* out and taken it up to the hill, between the three of us. Jennyfer walks around it, inspecting our work. With nothing more than the strength of her arms, she lifts it by the rear axle, pulling it back and forth, checking the structure. She is as confident in her body as Saioa is in her decisions. She puts it back on the ground and caresses the steel handles. Her eyes are shining. It must be a real joy to sit in the driver's seat, let it all go, and feel the wind in your face.

Jonás and Chris come with their helmets and we get them to keep an eye on the road, posting one at the top of the hill, and the other at the curve at the bottom. I've borrowed Michel's helmet. The kids come to check out our ride, some men are watching us from the social club. Seeing that we are girls, they call the others out from inside. We take our places. Jennyfer opens her legs, braces her feet on the front, and wraps the ropes around her wrists. I take my place in the middle, with my chest pressed against her. Saioa stands up at the back. 'Let's do it!' Jenny yells. I bend my knees and hold on tight to the handles on either side of me. I have never done anything like this before. Saioa starts running, pushing from behind, and the vibration of the bearings spreads throughout my body, my cheeks tingle. I feel Saioa jump aboard, crouching behind me, and then we are at the mercy of gravity. The lightness gives me uncontrollable vertigo, uncontrollable joy. I rest my head on Jennyfer's neck, I close my eyes, I hear screaming around me, the speed scares me. 'Left!' Saioa yells, and we automatically lean into the curve with the full weight of our existence. We are as one, and we are going downhill. I don't want to be anywhere else.

4

Before long, I'll be leaving here, but this will always be my river. Barely habitable, worn out, murky, with the gleam of the sun on the tribute of industry, old Icarus hanging from the bridge. I'm going to study journalism, in Bilbao. Soon, the past will close up like a wound, and the streets of the capital will overflow with life. But now, it's time to clean up.

There are about 30 people walking along the banks of the river. We're wearing sneakers, shorts and gloves, and carrying rubbish bags. The water is struggling to let go of four decades of industrial waste, domestic junk, rubbish that people throw off their balconies, and the mud that comes down from the mountains when it rains. Oihana and Lore are carrying an enormous parasol; the canvas is heavy with water, and they've called someone to help. 'It's been a while,' they greet me. We've dredged up plastic chairs and tables, tortoises from the Galapagos. Pieces of iron, steel rods, wheels, enormous, rusted washers, can all be found under the water. The logs form a natural dam, collecting debris, holding the water back. Two boys carry a tin sheet, the roof of a shed. There's Jenny, ripping off pieces of plastic that got caught in a tree the last time the river broke its banks. 'I shagged Jonás,' she confessed to me recently. She's staying here: she passed her exams; she still doesn't know if she will continue studying. We've pulled out benches, tables, scooters, phones, empty cans. Kaiet has found an old pram. Saioa whistles at me. She is pushing a shopping cart filled with debris, and yells: 'Want a beer?' Her mother's bar is right next to the river. She comes back with some cans.

The water licks at our ankles. It's smooth, and it shimmers. I don't really know anyone, nor do they me, but the calm generated by the group is as warm as the morning light. The ducks paddle at the mercy of the current. I spot a heron on the riverbank. Work, the work of freeing the river of human debris, for example, justifies a place in the group. Cleaning the river of its past so that the water flows freely.

Where the water runs at its deepest, we found a car engine. It was too heavy to move, even when we tied it up and tugged at it from the bank. We pull out car bumpers, windshield wipers, exhaust pipes, wing mirrors. I see Colomo: he's carrying a TV, the antennas outstretched, his trousers wet up to the thighs. Tomatoes ripen on the nearby balconies. Those in the water pull up bundles of sticks, empty petrol cans, and other pieces of junk, and hand them to those on the banks, who collect them from us. We hoist up the heavier debris by means of a pulley, from the bridge. A kid opens his hand and shows a girl from the *gaztetxe* the coins he has rescued from the mud. 'For the bumper cars,' he tells her. She runs off.

An oven, bike chains, floppy disks, video cassettes. *Ama* waves at me from the back window of the store, chucks me a *magdalena*. My aunt pokes her head out. They will close soon for the holidays. Paint tins, batteries, a bike. We sweat. We pass under the shadow of Icarus. The water that flows over us will be sea before nightfall.

Expandable Memory

Cristina Judar

Translated from Portuguese by Julia Sanches

This is how the day unfolded: as in the moment when the portable cosmos is recreated, there were unidentifiable objects strewn here and there, and various substances on the walls; numerous textures that gave rise to new and unimaginable creamy tones for use in hair, streaks, strands, faces, full existences, entire bodies. Neon-pink rivers stretched across the floor. The foam of the styling chairs—likely gutted with scissors and box cutters—was dusted in powdered lightener, in its usual turquoise hue, creating an unattractive watercolour tableau. To make matters worse, bottles of nail polish had been shattered and dumped on white towels of various sizes, rendering them impractical for conventional use.

The atmosphere in the beauty salon was tinged by what had taken place there, when nervous hands with wrinkled fingers sliced through the air in search of something indestructible to stop them. In the emptiness of the prevailing silence, there was the sound of 1,800 discordant symphonies; off-key trumpets, the choral whinnying of fiery steeds, wordless syllables slipping through paralysed lips. How many years of misfortune would be in store for whoever dared to break the mirrors that now reflected every angle of my den of beauty and entertainment, my den of vanity and secret-sharing?

I just wanted to know where my cleaning rags, dustpan, bucket, sponges, squeegee, bleach, and soap were. These weapons would bring an end to the chaos of scents and volatilities that had been purchased in bulk from a popular cosmetics store in the downtown area. But they were nowhere to be found. Even though I'd built that small world with my own two hands, there were no paths in sight, at least none that I could decipher.

Unsure of what to do, I sat in the only semi-unscathed chair in the room and watched Ricardo, Ohanna, Fátima, Clarice, Rogério, Nelson, and Dona Norma working intensely. In under a week, they were able to able to get my own private sanctuary back in working order. Water once again flowed and white lather bubbled; the space filled with perfume. Some things were fixed while others, broken beyond repair, were replaced. Unidentifiable parts of previously intact objects were tossed out, products were ordered, the walls took on new hues, the floor was once again fertile ground. As all this happened, it was as if I was being given a much-wanted second skin. Which was more or less how I felt, too. The collective action of these people who were important to me in different ways and played various roles in my life helped me rehabilitate a body that was both home and temple, breadwinner and site of fun and belonging.

*

Moments before I found out what had happened at the salon, someone came to visit. It was Fátima, my loyal neighbour and customer. She was on her way home from the market with a bounty of fruit worthy of Alceu Valença, which she usually brought as a gift or an offer that I couldn't refuse:
 that summer morning, it was as if a profusion of voices were spiralling up to the sky, making words difficult to parse and sharpening colours and senses. The peels, the colours, the fruit juice, the gaze, the desire, the flesh, the skin, the slurping, the exhale, rope tobacco, the holes, the thread, the cheese and plants, the blue silk around peach fuzz, the apple, the women old and young, the shortcut of the girl walking home from school, the catcall, the disgust and disrepute, the waste, the leftovers, the rats, the

pigeons, the busted crates, the traveling dogs, the derailed oranges, the slippery grapes, the amber oil, the effervescent pastes, the one- two- three- coloured squares, the slices, the sting, the sweet, the sour, the bitter and the raw, the bargain, the papaya, the hand, the breast, the coin, the cost, the promise, the softened, the joke, the offer, the kick, the bite, the slip, the bananas—ripe, their spots—the pulp, the drink, the sap, the looks, the saliva, the scream, the whistle, the nails, the boys, the zap, the old men, the pirated DVDs, the gutter tomatoes, the seeds, the scowl, the swivel, the whistles, the pants, the shirts, the laces, the flip-flops, the immigrants, the radios, the necklaces, the earrings, the rings, the buckles, the dresses, the batteries, the shorts, the retirees, the canvas, the newsstand, the sharpener, the blind man, the violinist, the parrot, the cobbles, the clash of the shopping carts, the grocery bags, the newspapers, the squeegees, the brooms, the pot lids, the right-wing nuts, the bouquets, the laces, the eggs, the conserves, the collard greens, the beans, the democrats, the potatoes, the peppers, the packages, the four for the price of one, the half-dozens, the units, the dish towels, the grub, the wash-basin, the scale, the shuffle, the theft, the fibres, the cheap honey, the skin, the spices, the kilo, the ballots, the bills, the change, the holler, the laughter, the smile, the pretty girls can't have their fruit and eat it too.

Fátima stood at the salon door and lifted her hand to her mouth at the sight of the tragic scene in front of her. Then she took out her phone and made a few urgent calls.

*

It was quiet on the Saturday before the riot. The salon wasn't too full, so after giving everything a once-over, I went out to see my dear Ricardo, an ogã[3] at the neighbourhood ilê. There was a party once a month at the terreiro, where the rituals were celebrated. It always ended around ten in the evening. Even after being on my feet for hours at work, I could still connect with the people who gathered there and I could still follow the orixás dancing, each with their unique, resonant thrum.

*

Tum tu tata, tum tutu tatata... tum tu tata, tum tutu tatata (and so on and so forth).

As the collective dancing body moved in a circular, cyclical procession, the atabaques set the rhythm for the hearts, arms, and steps of the community gathered in the large tent. Amid the flowers, fruit, plants, and flames of the main

---

3 A Candomblé priest

altar, the devotion symbolized by colours and mingling perfumes warmed the heads of all those present.

All you needed to feel the vibrations in the air was to be alive:

head is voice, calabash is dress, petals in action, howls flow through veins, ocean waves stir up sand, winds whip around the peak, sword sits at the shoulder of the iaô, short burst of rain, long steam, dense weeds, smooth earth, salty tears, sweat hanging in the air, long-awaited rose, breakthrough lightning, knot-binding fire, arrow in flight, eye afloat, atomic tooth, exposed nail bed, occult symbols, hummed point, a woman's folding fan, threshed corn, alert nipple, the metal worker's current, bone of dug-up earth, wooden spear, arm of river mouth, mermaid song, cicada screech, moonlight, coloured scarves, voices orchestrating melodies, morning dew, goosebumps, time in heat, magisterial globe, ritual baquetas, a sound leaves one mouth and enters another, lips in volume and heat, fuchsia-red, stars in clamour, potent limb, Roma wheel, gossip and cards, trident and fork, soldier on patrol, valiant gesture, top hat, silver-moon bracelet, goldsmiths' inscription, one baby in arms, another who doesn't know she exists, an unknown tune, New Guinea walking stick, Jamaican chili pepper, black-eyed peas, leaping lynx, coral snake, young sun, copper wires, rainbow, golden snake, buffalo, snail, goat, acarajé, abará, dendê oil, arch, shield and spear, lavender, white lace, muddled herbs, green water, brocade, palm leaf, straw hat, bamboo grove, amulet and stone, mud, sand, mirror, shell-shaped hand, juice of fruit, queen's crown, see-through branches, drop of milk, rock sap, hazy cotton, interrupted plot, shepherd's crook, song, basil, gimcrack, okra, corn flour, clay bowl, herb of grace, sole of foot, dust, hollow, reset.

*

As the ialorixá conducted the various phases of the ritual, Ricardo was the man I loved. He helped set the rhythm of that sacred place. It was a beautiful thing to see gesture and sound becoming a single entity, an organism of faith and power born from the roots of the earth. His presence inspired me to beat my own path, to understand and carve out a space for myself in the day-to-day insanity of São Paulo.

*

I came here three years ago from Redenção, a town in the eastern part of the state. I wanted to travel around the world, so I moved to a big city whose prefabricated but versatile—or rather, hovering—terrain contained unlimited pathways. I earned my living the same way I had in my hometown, by tending to women's well-being and beauty.

I'd been renting a room from Dona Norma ever since moving to the city, and she eventually agreed to let me use her garage in exchange for a share of the salon's profits. First I cleaned and refurbished the space, confident in the possibility of a fresh start. Time passed and I acquired things like cosmetics, tools, equipment, and furniture with the money I brought in. My client list grew, and every object I purchased was like another piece of the sanctuary I was building for myself. Together, those women and I were the painted deities of that grey city, even though we didn't know this.

Now that I was far from the narrow-mindedness of my hometown, where everyone knew me and where I was from, I started daydreaming about going back to school again. Though still out of the reach, my plan to enter higher education no longer felt impossible.

*

My birth name is Caio but I've always felt like more of a Susana, which has never been straightforward or easy to figure out. Especially if you were born into a conservative family at the end of the world—in a land of cattle and

bullwhips, large barbecue lunches, boisterous laughter, stigma, legacy, and generational feuds:
 the meat, the hunt, the dagger, the land, the fence, the tired jokes, the rage, the smiles, the leap, the sweat and the hair, the coveting, the judging, the cutting, the court, the blow, the bawl, the fist, the baiting, the shirt and pants, the chrome buckle, the saddle, the stirrup, the bullwhip, the wide brims, the beer pooled in the gullet, the belly, the rot, the itchy balls, the spittle, the cum, the spur, he's a fag, he's a sissy, somebody should kill him, he needs to die, not in my house, not here, never, my wife would never, my son wouldn't dream of it, a moment of weakness, all kinds of stuff happens around these parts, compadre, accomplice, we shake on things here, no need for pens or paper, this land is ours, trespass and we'll shoot, folks like that have got no place in this town, men are men, women are women, boys are boys, girls are girls, by force is necessary, I won't have it, he's no son of mine, God won't have it, where in the world, a stain on the family name, the shame, the indecency, male, female, acting like a gentleman, humiliation for generations to come, our great-grandparents came here by boat, they ate the bread the devil kneaded, never complained, calloused hands, blistered fingers, Monday to Monday in the fields, sunrise to sundown, deathly thin, 14 kids, three dead, one midwife in the whole

town, no anaesthesia, delivered by the light of an oil lamp, God save her, tears of blood, four chickens, one donkey, the piglet died, the hoarse rooster, the skeletal cow, mouth-watering, the thin porridge ladled with a wooden spoon, all in a row, you learn by the belt, no such thing as psychology, pants dropped and belts got, kneeling in the cornfields, hand to the rod, the crown of thorns, the burden of responsibility, the bell, grandfather broke his back to open that warehouse, those first years were crushing, now the missus complains, I do what I can, everyone is on track, except for him, a terrible loss, I bet we're being punished, God is good but he's no fool, he takes from the unworthy, from where I stand it's like he never existed, he moved to São Paulo, we never speak his name, a dead name, a dead person, wiped from our memories, moved to the back of beyond, vanished, thank God, I'm a man of honour, I'm a woman of faith, God-fearing, family is everything to me, when judgment comes my soul will be clean, I lay my head on the pillow and sleep through the night, the talk is good, someone put the kettle on, she brought some cake to have with the coffee.

*

Ricardo's mother, Armanda, was a regular at the salon. She accidentally instigated our first meeting. It happened one day when I was busy with a dye job. He came by the salon to bring his mother her glasses, which she'd left at home. Awkward and polite, he excused himself. I said, come in and he smiled. Oh, honey, I'm lucky my head is attached to my neck. You're not wrong. You're an angel. Bye. Bye, Mom. A pleasure. The pleasure's all mine. He turned around. There were sparks in my eye.

*

We met again during my first visit to the ilê. My friend Clarice had been going for years and took me with her. I had no idea he would be there, let alone that he'd have such an important role to play in that space reserved for drummers. He looked beautiful dressed all in white, with colourful necklaces, singing with his eyes closed, hands drumming out the sacred rhythms. He brought the heavens down to earth.

The ritual ended, he waved, then came to say hello. Hi, how are you? It's so beautiful here. You like it? I love it, the energy is amazing. It really is, and strong too. I'm impressed. Come back again. We'd love to have you.

I went back as often as I could. For the place, which did me good and accepted me for who I was. For him, who did me good and accepted me for who I was. Our conversations grew longer and more interesting. Eventually, we added each other on social media. On one of my days off, we went out for coffee. We kissed. We were together for the first time. Since then, we've been going steady. The one thing he was scared of was how his mother would react when she found out about us and, to be fair, I was scared of that too.

That's how our relationship went. Clarise was the only person who knew about us. We were a hidden treasure, which was good in a lot of ways. I had so many other secrets that were painful; at least for now, I didn't mind having a secret that did me good.

*

After I moved here, I got to experience nightlife in São Paulo—one of the craziest and most scintillating in the world, I'd been told—with Ohanna, who claimed to have the same traits as the city:

all girls are beautiful under neon lights, but what's up with this line?, don't start, get moving, these heels won't do, ay, I don't give a shit about him, just pretend, I did the Egyptian, it's gratis until 12 tonight, run, it's starting to drizzle, I desperately need a touch-up, where's the snow, I forgot to buy smokes, look at all these people!, the smell of piss, tobacco, ash, embers, cigarette butts, pass the joint, the cherry won't stop going out, the strap keeps slipping, the bra cup, the scratchy lace, Chanel bob, Chanel perfume, from Paraguay, the bag is from 25 de março, jaguar or panther?, neither, the print is tiger, vinyl clothes give me goosebumps, I absolutely love corselets, black lipstick slaps, golden mouth, emerald-green belly, sphinx-like posture, cracked Maravilha nail polish, varnished with tiny silver stars, velvet is life, they ran by and knocked into me, the friction, look at all these people!, what a pain, hot breath, total douche, that asshole acted like he couldn't see me, it's fake, bitch, how do I fill out my top lip? I wouldn't dream of overlining at the salon, I can't miss this tune, the dancefloor is practically dead, it's early, follow me, look, a spinning globe, a mirrored wall, a red-velvet sofa tanned with sunrise cachaça, flamingo chandelier, mahogany balcony with marble detailing, seismic shock, you got beer all over me, sorry, it's okay, quit looking so miserable, have fun, you'll be dry in no time, flashbacks, a bunch of old geezers, worse than Redenção, the night is young, smoke lounge, let's go, red-berry vodka caipirinha, passionfruit sake caipirinha, a wooden stirrer, grab me a napkin, put them both on my tab please, the start of the night is always lame, I love dancefloors, let's dance, *'cause I'm free to do what I want*, this is super 90s, next it'll be Corona, the queen who sings *This is the rhythm of the night*, ah, help me, bitch, better have a sandwich outside, synthetic fabric soaks up the hot stink, the hot-dog stand is next to the guy with the Styrofoam, right, you're going for the Corote, haha, blue Corote makes the soul levitate, all heavenlike, Angélica, listen to that banger, put your cell in your panties, your bra, somewhere safe, look at where we are woman, it's a sea of Ubers, a line of Santa Cecilia residents, green, blue, and yellow karaoke, hey hot stuff, doll, beautiful, are you taken?, got a light?, sure do.

*

I spoke with Nelson at one of the schools in the neighbourhood after watching him give a talk about how literature can liberate and transform people and reality. Books had played an important part in my life, and I wanted to be an arts teacher, so he and I swapped some ideas after the event:

a line that evokes sound and fire, the order of the universe, spiky brush strokes in lukewarm hues, tags, graffiti, how to incentivise critical thinking, scarlet liquid, consciousness multiplied to the nth degree, an end to subpar conditions, children deprived of safety gates, toys, and essence-destroying clothes, stories repeated until they take on new dimensions, tales of sound, peace, and fury, active citizenship, residents represented

Expandable Memory

by magisterial screens, disencumbered creativity, revolutionary realities, recovery of identity, existences that add meaning to life, poles flipped helter-skelter, independent creators of territorial directions, high-and-mighty sunflowers, the classic house-with-tree-chimney-gate-cloud-sun drawing as a site of breakage, days of lush seas and skies, high tides, palms on gentle soil, ruminant trees of future stories, students of the earth, brothers of the moon, children of fire and light, asteroids composed of speed and intention, the merits of untimely figures, lightning drawn on rock, droplets of rain on a millimetric course, wonderfully deformed modelling clay, half-empty pages of words that have yet to be spoken, a dynamic language forged in the image and likeness of bodies, fables in gestation, dominoes of advertised countdown, multichromatic watercolours, affective scintillations, arrows of mutual understanding, exchange circles, a string of little flags, children and adults like entire cells, brochures, slits, scratches, origami, collage, posters, letters, diaries, crêpe paper, full bloom, disseminating potential, various understandings, retrograde waves in dissolution, hymns in absolution, loose books, dry leaves as references for much-wanted forms, jumping bubbles, multithemed comics, strips in uncommon sagas, all the stories, maps and gestures of a possible, much freer future.

Come again sometime. We can talk about college-entrance exams and some areas of study that could be of interest to you, the professor suggested.

*

'Suzaninha, darling, when Rosa is done with my feet, will you wash my hair with that shampoo I love?'

'Of course, Dona Armanda.'

The sweet and fruity, floral-scented extract penetrated Dona Armanda's capillary jungle as my fingers slid intensely through the warm, slippery atmosphere and evenly applied product to the strands, pathways, and forests tangled with ideas that she said aloud, eyes shut to keep the soap out:

he's good, amazing, my pride and joy, studious and dedicated, he hasn't introduced us to a girlfriend yet, it's only a matter of time, he's shy, took after his dad and grandfather, but one thing I really can't stand is seeing him mixed up in all this macumba and terreiro nonsense, I've already asked him to stop, we've never experienced anything this shameful in the family, it's pai this, mãe that, but from where I stand you can only have one mother and father, people at the terreiro want to destroy the pillar of society, to discredit it, then there's the irmãos de barco, that's something I heard him say the other day, *boat brothers*, but what boat?, it's got to be one of those Styrofoam boats they use for work on rivers or in the ocean, in waterfalls or streams, it must be, as if people with no blood relation can become family from one second to the next, as if you could wake up one day and decide, this man is my brother now, this woman is my mother, and this man is my father, it's ludicrous, an affront, they even ask their new mães and pais to bless them, if this kind of thing had happened back in my day, it would've caused a scandal with heads rolling and leather bring eaten, there'd be no stone left unturned, and speaking of leather, I found out he plays atabaque by accident one day when Ricardinho was out and Rogério, a childhood friend, knocked on the door with a tall drum, hi Dona Armanda, is Ricardo home? he said, I had to bring Ricardo's instrument home because there's some work being done on our rehearsal space, I can come pick it up later or he can bring it back next week, at the saída de santo, we still have to practice for it, thanks Dona Armanda, tell him I sent him a message on WhatsApp but since he didn't see it and I was short on time, I thought I'd just bring it to him, Mom and Dad are well, thank God, and I say, sure, leave it here, I'll be seeing you, look after yourself, Dona Armanda, see you later! and I even had to haul that huge drum wrapped in ropes and stinking of herb-smoke with my own two arms, I'd do anything for my son, anything to see him get away from all that, from all that dirty macumba claptrap, that mingling of people, blacks and whites, whites and blacks, men who want to be women, women who want to be men, dykes, fags, potheads, thugs, hoodlums, transvestites, they'll take anyone, there are no rules or regulations, flesh is king, just the thought of a man like that gives me goosebumps, a queer in a lacy skirt and rainbow necklace taking advantage of my darling boy, all kinds of things go down there, all kind of things come up, female demons, male demons, it's all cackles, curses, debauchery, they drink cachaça with tridents tucked under their arms, eat farofa, they use faith as a cover to let in things that are far worse, to get close, to smell the back of his neck, grope his body, rub up on him. What if he touched the beard or lipstick of the man pretending to be a woman?, I'm a woman, I was born a woman, men have dicks, women have pussies, pants, dresses, dear God, please get those images out of my head, that's all I ask, what harm have I done, the water is perfect, Susaninha, go ahead and douse my whole head, the temperature is perfect too, lather it in, sink in your fingers, may the water free me, may the water return me, white water that tastes white, growing shampoo foam, the floral and fruity scent makes me feel relieved and protected, may the water save me so that I emerge purer, wash my entire head, I want to be free from all this, from the drum, the leather, the animal body that surrendered a strip of its skin for my son to beat, from the taste of Ricardinho's cum in the mouth of a man wearing a skirt, I bet he'd swallow it, I bet that man would feel like more of a woman than I do, more like a woman, more than me, thanks, you can shut off the water now and wrap my head in a white towel. This is why I always come back, the service is impeccable, you're the best hairdresser I've met in my life.

*

Right then, it was as if the outskirts of my soul held all of the pain that I couldn't accommodate:
   the animal lament, the curved journey of the poor, the shadow that roams the neighbourhood with a metal bucket on its head, the shadow that does not know if it is person or apparition, the bucket as a heart ripped out of the chest, the cat trapped in the gutter, the fumigation that corrodes eyes and ears, the abrupt flap of virginal wings, the unending repetition until the moment the parrot finally parrots the joke, the bird-joke likes on Instagram, the minor-celebrity bird, the bull on its way to the abattoir, a thwack or two, the chaos, the blind rat going round and round until it collapses, the nausea before the heart stops,

the tarantula on the cusp of death, the vulture circling in sight for a few cuts, the scorpion amid flames, the solitary old man, the memory of a night of hot food, tangled family conversation, the baby awaiting affection, the absence of affection, the dog caught in the undertow, a grey wall as the only view, the cold, the fear, the hunger, the night, the unfairly clubbed bat, the sick man who wishes in vain to travel, the misunderstood man who just want friends, a table crowded with people, the eye that reflects the flame, a room of people standing vigil around a coffin, an infant with no warm-blooded company, the salt stuffed in the eyes of a pig, the apple shoved down its throat, the sure-fire dagger, the sharpened blade, the inflamed muscles, animal gut as a snack for the rich, painful flesh served in thin slivers, the shootout that strikes mother and son in the belly, the unwanted blow, the bruised skin, the burst artery, the decomposing nails, a profusion of pus, a fetid smell, the mouldy buildings, the hole, the hoarse, the rusted box cutter, humidity affects the lungs, the excised halo, the two scars, the two holes, the grey matter in the sky, the threadbare veils, the high-pitched tweet, the roar, the burp, the head beating incessantly, the exorcism, the abomination that is a strange body, my leather-waste, my undesired core, my inappropriate existence, my organism with no proper place, my dungeon a sin, fingers buried in deep-water seaweed, in the acid jungle, in the graveyard clay, the softened roots, the malodorous entrails, the voice that suits no choir, the religious abomination, the family curse, the longing to flee pain, the pain, no end in sight.

*

Dona Armanda swaggered and showed off, white towel wrapped around her head like a turban. As I picked up the hair dryer and brush so I could finish the job as quickly as possible, I got a text from Clarice:
Ricardinho asked me to tell you he'll meet you at the terreiro. Tonight's the saída das yabas, we're bringing fruit, honey, and white flowers in gratitude. Dress up, but don't take long. Text or call when you've left?
My enthusiasm was mostly gone. My movements felt slow and I had this partial blindness that sent me into autopilot, making me even more uncomfortable. But I'd go, of course I would, I needed more than ever to be with my people.

*

Ricard was very late to the yabás ceremony. He grabbed his things and ran like crazy to the terreiro. They were probably already waiting. Despite the rush, the ritual started on time and went on as usual. As soon as it was over, Ricardo hugged the people closest to him, asked for a blessing from ialorixá, helped get things in order, said goodbye to his fellow ogãs, and walked toward Susana and Clarice. He immediately slid his hand into his pocket and then zipped open his backpack.

His cellphone was not in his pant pocket, let alone in his backpack. It lay forgotten on his bedroom dresser and vibrated with every new message. The unusual commotion drew Dona Armanda's attention. She was walking down the hallway when she registered the unexpected presence of her son's phone and of every chapter, housed in 64 gigabytes of expandable memory, of the love story of Ricardo and Susana.

Dry and Green

Nesrine Khoury

Translated from Arabic by Jonathan Wright

In the story the dove picked up an olive branch in its beak and flew to Noah's Ark with it. It was carrying something that would become part of my life, part of the heritage of my family and the reason for the train journey I am now embarking on.

But I must confess, I have long preferred crows to doves, and I don't think the stories have done the crows justice. I even like their cawing. One of them used to visit my bedroom window in the village and I saw it as my friend. The day Jawan first kissed me, I heard it cawing in the distance and that was the sound of love. The day I left the village for the last time I didn't see it. Maybe, like me, the crow wanted to turn things upside down.

It's a new November. I won't see Jawan. It's a new November and Jawan's veined hands are wrapped around another woman's waist in the afternoon, when we used to meet.

That's what I told myself when the steward from the train company came past giving out earphones. Inside me I felt an urge to hear some of those songs we used to hear on those days when we went to harvest the olives in the family's grove in the village. I took a set of earphones from the pleasant woman in her grey uniform, which was ironed more neatly than necessary. I thought she should tone down her smile a little, out of respect for the sadness brought on by the flood of memories that came over me in the train. Or is unjustified sadness just an Oriental trait? Maybe that was it.

With a single turn of my head, I can scan the world of work, technology and social media that engrossed the other passengers in my carriage. I seem to be the only person with my head leaning back on the headrest to watch the hills rush past outside the window, evoking another flood of memories.

Going to Grandfather's house in the village was something we looked forward to throughout the year. We would check the calendar and note the official holidays and religious feasts, and finally my father would rev up the car engine, and off we would go.

But in November we didn't need the calendar on the wall, and holidays were not a factor in the timing. It was Grandfather and the olive harvest that decided when we would go to the village.

At the time it never occurred to me that one of my ancestors was one of those feudalists vilified in our schoolbooks, the feudalists we insulted in our essays with such enthusiasm in order to obtain high marks in exams. This was a country that wanted its socialist ideas reflected in the sinuously scripted writings of its schoolchildren.

My grandfather wasn't evil and he didn't own the village, but he did have extensive olive groves and orchards of fruit trees. I don't know where the idea came to me from, but when I was young, I thought my grandfather was really one of those olive trees, but that instead of emerging from the ground, he had turned up in a cradle by mistake. But he never forgot where he came from, and he spent his whole life consorting with his fellow olive trees and looking after them like a brother. When he grew older, the wrinkles on his face looked like the trunk of an olive tree. 'It's in his genes,' I said.

I never saw Grandfather cry, but I'm confident that if he had done so, his tears would have been the finest extra virgin olive oil in the whole world.

Although the groves were Grandfather's, their bounty belonged to everyone who worked in them, and that's a genuinely socialist idea, my dear social studies textbook.

Every year, dozens of families and individuals volunteered to join us in the olive harvesting. All they needed to do was tell my grandmother in the early summer, or they could just turn up when the season began, and my grandmother would then cheerfully add their names to the annual olive ledger. Then they became official partners in the harvesting and would receive their share when the olives and the oil were divided up.

I loved taking part in all the rituals of the harvest – helping my grandmother organise the ledger, joining the children later in picking olives off the ground, and in all the tasks that suited the age and height I had reached when the season came round.

In Grandfather's groves the olive picking wasn't something people did just for payment in money or in kind. It was like an annual village carnival, and it provided us with fun and pleasure as well as the olives we harvested. We ended up like the farmers in our reading books, happy after a long day's work. That isn't just a socialist myth. Sometimes farmers really do smile, forgetting their back pains, the hardships of life and their mounting debts.

Grandfather would call me 'the little farmer girl', or sometimes 'the olive princess' or 'the tea queen' or 'the local radio', depending on the job I was doing. I liked all these titles, though I did sometimes grumble when I was sent to the kitchen to help the women prepare meals and make pots of tea for the workers. I preferred to stay outside, where there was singing and young men with rippling muscles.

As season succeeded season, I came to have friends that I called my 'olive friends'. We would gather every season. We grew up together and saw olive saplings grow into full trees as the groves expanded and the number of pickers increased. We kept in touch with each other by means that varied according to our ages and developments in society and technology – firstly through home telephone numbers and postal addresses, later through mobile phones and, in the more recent seasons, through social media accounts. Yet it was still unusual for anyone to contact others after the season had ended and everyone had gone back to their ordinary lives. There seemed to be an implicit agreement that our friendships applied only in Grandfather's olive groves. But that has not yet prevented me from being eager to maintain my links with all of them. There's a mysterious sense of safety in the idea that they are there in case I need them. This friendship is like the trunk of an olive tree that I could cling to one day when I'm at a loss as to what to do, and feel I've been left alone to drown.

Our gang or group didn't have a leader, although I was well-placed to take on that role, as the daughter of the landowning family; as the person who in some seasons oversaw the ledger; and as someone who knew my way around the kitchen, where to find bottles of cold water, and the secret hiding places for snacks and titbits. Although my personality was right for such a role, I tried as hard as possible not to take it on. It might have made me popular in the real world but a pariah in the schoolbooks.

To be honest, throughout the years I lived in Syria, moving between the town and the village, and later living in the capital, I didn't find a better or more obvious contemporary model of social solidarity, of working together for the common good, than harvesting season in Grandfather's olive groves. Without making any claims, it was a real example in practice of the principle that the land should belong to those who cultivate it and work on it.

There's a film on now, on the screen in the train, and neither I nor any of the other passengers in my carriage seem interested in watching it. It's probably an American film dubbed in Spanish, and although it's rather difficult to make such judgments these days, most people in the world now dress, eat, drink, and make films the American way. I'm amused by the idea that I am talking to myself and giving opinions that sound judicious, as if I have borrowed Grandfather's tongue and his way of explaining the world. I could have listened to him for hours and hours without tiring or getting bored, ignoring every temptation to go and play with the other children outside or watch cartoons on television. I am almost certain that whatever I have acquired in the way of general knowledge, and mental skills for dealing with the things that life throws in my way, came to me through that man, and not from schoolbooks. I even imitated his taste in books to read, and I started to create the outlines of my library according to Grandfather's preferences. That means that ancient Arabic poetry holds pride of place, then books on ideas and politics and, no less importantly to him, magazines on agronomy. He was always eager to keep track of the latest research and he was one of the first people, and part of a small minority in his age group, to own a computer and explore the world of the Internet, to keep up with everything new in the fields that interested him. My grandfather was ahead of his time, without leaving his village. But I could never match his amazing memory for poems, which he recited whenever the moment was right in the flow of a conversation. I was also incapable of acquiring his ability to diagnose the ailments of trees and the best way to treat them, and, most importantly, neither I nor anyone else in the family inherited his seductive eloquence when he spoke.

Olive trees are temperamental, and even Grandfather's experience and skills could not come up with a convincing scientific explanation for poor olive harvests. When I was young and I asked him why the olive harvest was so poor in one particular year, he would say, 'Even trees get tired and discontented, just like us. This year they're not in a good enough mood to produce a large harvest, and we humans shouldn't bother them or hold it against them or blame them. If they want to take a break, so be it. That's their right. But, trust me, next year they'll make up the difference many times over.' Of course, I trusted him, for everything my grandfather said was an indubitable truth. Besides, I saw him as one of those trees, understanding the way they thought and the vicissitudes of their lives, and maybe also talking to them in some secret language, who knows? And they did indeed make up the difference many times over the following year.

In those poor seasons the mood in the village was rather sad because it might mean a loss of livelihood for some of the workers who were paid wages, or low stocks of oil and olives in the kitchens of the families who took part in the harvesting. Sometimes they would have to buy olive oil from faraway places, which was expensive for many people. But the olive festival never stopped, however bad things were. The rituals were always the same, and Grandfather and the other men in the family were careful to arrange matters in such a way that none of their workers lost any of their income. Grandmother never turned away anyone who wanted to take part, and she filled the pages of the ledger for the year with names, whether repeated from the previous year or new ones. I think that ledger is an important historical document that could be relied upon to study the families in the area, their characteristics and living conditions, as well as the effects of climate, technological, and political change, both locally and internationally, on the presence, movement and cohesion of those families.

Jawan's name went into the olive ledger only once. Then he kissed me and went away, leaving in my heart love of a kind that seems out of tune with the way the world is now. Instead it's something better suited to the 1980s or 1990s that I used to hear about and make fun of, its songs and its films and its horrible romances – an enduring, enervating, tormenting love that leaves the butterflies in your stomach unsatisfied and permanently aflutter, a love that never falls asleep whatever time zone it happens to be in, reliant on a biological clock that can't tell night from day.

My friends in the olive gang didn't like Jawan, and he too didn't show any desire to be one of them. His individualism was overpowering and didn't suit the communal spirit that came over us during the olive festival. We left our individualism at home and closed the door firmly on it before coming. That was the crux of the matter. I don't know whether this idea comes from my own analysis or deductions or whether it's one of my grandfather's ideas, a distillation of his long experience.

The only thing was that Jawan didn't have quite enough money to cover the costs of his journey and the olive season happened to come around, open to all comers, and so he volunteered. As simply as that, a pure coincidence swept away my heart. Maybe love has always been that way – a chronological game that I end up losing.

Jawan didn't understand that the olive gang and I were not copies of each other, as he once described us. There wasn't any coercion of any kind whatsoever, either religious, political, or social, that forced us to set aside our individuality and come to work and melt into the group. In fact, friendship alone was our motivation – friendship that takes when it gives, friendship that was eventually crushed by everyday life and dissipated when we went back home to rediscover our individuality in readiness to wrestle with the modern world.

The train company woman announced that the train was approaching my station, so I had to leave my thoughts of Jawan and Grandfather in the olive groves, sort out my modest luggage and prepare to get off the train. The air outside was hot enough to make one long for a cold beer. I sat at a table on the terrace at the nearest café and asked the waitress for a *jarra de cerveza* – the Spanish term for a large glass of beer. The word reminded me, with good reason, of an Arabic *jarra*, one of those large ceramic jars that sat in the corner of Grandmother's kitchen and held the sweetest cold water I have ever tasted.

The waitress brought me a plate of olives as tapas, a light meal that can be either cold or hot, and that cafés and restaurants are famous for offering in Spain in general and especially in Andalusia, where in some towns they come free of charge when you order a drink.

All over the world olives go well with drinks. In our country they are not just decorative or served as snacks. They are an essential part of the meal at breakfast and at dinner. Our kitchens are never without jars of green or black olives, or wrinkled *attoun* olives, as part of the year's provisions. I once unthinkingly told a European friend of mine that I put olives in a *labneh* sandwich, sprinkled dried mint on it and poured a little olive oil on it, then ate it with a cup of tea for breakfast. Almost every word in my narrative amazed her. '*Labneh*? In a sandwich? With olives? And salt? And oil? And tea? Really?'

I didn't know how to translate the term *qatf al-labneh*, the common expression for the process of making *labneh* at home. Cheesecloth bags full of full-fat yoghurt, hanging over the sink to let the water drain away until the yoghurt turns into *labneh*, were a permanent feature of Grandmother's kitchen, and of most kitchens in the village. In Spain I tried to make *labneh* from the plain Greek yoghurt I found in the supermarket. I drained off the water and put a piece of sterilised cheesecloth over the top of it. Sometimes I succeeded and the taste was rather delicious, but I wouldn't dare to call this simple process *qatf al-labneh*.

The olive season doesn't end as soon as the harvesting work is done and suitable olives are sent to the olive press. After that, the women gather, wash the rest of the olives set aside as food, crush them with stones or cut them with knives, then pack them with salt, water, oil and slices of lemon inside glass jars. These would then be shared out fairly between all those who took part in the work.

I remember that on a tour of an olive press in a village near the Andalusian town of Baeza in the Jaén region, the region best known for producing olives and olive oil, I asked the guide, who was the son of the owner, what the criteria were for choosing which olives to keep for eating. He was surprised by the question and didn't understand it at first. Then he told me that most of the olives were sent for pressing and only a small amount, maybe enough for a small jar, was left for the family, if they wanted.

On one of the walls in the olive press in Andalusia, there was a large map of the world, with coloured pins showing where visitors to the press had come from. The guide was proud that the business his father had set up in that small village was now known in faraway parts of the world. At the time I remembered my grandfather and the rotating globe in his study. He knew the world through books, and he spoke to me time and again about the journey that olive trees had made around the world and why they flourished in particular areas rather than others. He used to say that when you give to olive trees, they give back. 'Like love?' I asked. He laughed and said that I clearly took after my grandmother. In fact, I hadn't noticed that at the time.

Although Grandfather was comfortably well off, in good health and vigorous, he had never thought of travelling abroad, even to visit his children or his siblings. When I asked him why, he asked me to come for a walk. We went towards the 'mother tree', the oldest tree in his grove and in the whole area, thought to be a thousand years old. You can see us gathered around it in every photograph of family occasions. He told me that the family had an ancient tradition that if any member of the family left the country, they had to take a cutting from the tree with them and plant it in the country where they settled. He also told me that the family had lost contact with one of his uncles after he travelled abroad and the last they heard of him was that he was in the Iberian peninsula, probably in Spain. Then he continued to explain his idea: this tree had never left the village, but it didn't need to do so in order to travel, either as a cutting, as oil, or as laurel soap. Some of us had to stay put for the good of the community.

At the time I thought that we used to gather around Grandfather in the photographs and I got a little confused. Which of them was a thousand years old, with roots sunk deep in the ground?

For Grandmother and the village women, the meetings and preparations for the olive season began some time before the season actually started. They gathered regularly to prepare the sheets that were spread out under the trees during the picking to collect the olives. They also had to sew the sacks in which they put the olives and took them to the presses. Grandmother had precise specifications and high standards of cleanliness for the sheets and the way they were made, the quality of the cloth and the thread that was used, and the right level of ventilation that the sacking allowed to the olives. She calculated everything – the number of trees, the approximate number of olives each tree would yield that year, the size of the olives, how many of them each sack would hold and the number of sacks that would be needed.

Grandmother loved abundance and her main concern was that people should feel comfortable and at ease, but that meant she had to have everything under control and leave no room for unpleasant surprises.

I liked to look out on the olive groves from the balcony of the house when the preparations for the harvest were underway and before the pickers had arrived. Seen from above, it looked like a fine painting, and it would never occur to anyone who saw it that the colours and designs on the sheets were random. They would probably conclude that everything was as carefully prepared as a long take in a film by Theo Angelopoulos. But when the people arrived it would be more like a scene from an Italian film, with laughter and chatter, bustle, and plenty of food.

The guide on the tour of the olive press in Andalusia insisted that Spanish olives were distinct from the Italian variety. In the village too we always tried to highlight the ways in which our oil and our olives were distinct from those from other areas. When there was a poor harvest, my grandmother would say: 'They might have a better season than us this year, but here we're never short of love, and who knows what kind of love they have there?' Of course, people in other areas probably weren't short of love either, but this kind of rivalry is normal, whether in a forgotten Middle Eastern village or in the country that produces the most oil and wins international prizes for quality.

Making this journey wasn't part of my plans. I've been in Madrid for some months to finish my course, but a dinner with a friend changed everything. On our table, as on any table in any Spanish restaurant, there was a small bottle of olive oil and, as usual, the first thing I did was ask for a small piece of bread so that I could drip some of the oil onto it and taste it, and prove to myself that the oil in Grandfather's house was the best in the world. I don't know why, where the pressing need to confirm this came from.

But at that dinner something strange happened: the oil had that same taste, the taste I remembered, the winning taste. I drank some water and had another taste, but the taste was the same: the taste of home.

I remembered Grandfather's lost uncle and the olive cutting he took on his journey. I asked the restaurant management where the oil came from, but no one was sure because they bought various kinds of oil from numerous shops. Given that Andalusia is the biggest olive oil producer, I decided to start a process of investigation from there, and I went on a tour of an olive press with people from China, Ireland, and Sweden. I tasted various kinds of oil and heard the guide explain things that I already knew by heart. I bought bottles of oil of all the kinds they produce, but none of them tasted anything close to the taste of the oil in Grandfather's house.

I admitted to myself that what I was doing was rather crazy. Maybe this alleged family tradition was just a myth that grandfather liked to tell me to amuse me. Grandfather's uncle couldn't possibly still be alive, and what good would his family be to me, even if they existed? Or to anyone?

But in fact, I was looking for myself. I was looking for myself in the faces of the people who looked like me in some way that I didn't realise. I was looking for a tree in which I could see myself, in the same way as I had seen Grandfather's face in that ancient family tree in the village. I wanted the journey to track the course of my life in my own way, but maybe I wanted this tree to take me back to the land of my grandfather, who had also traced his own journey there.

I learned to cook in Grandmother's kitchen. I was pampered in my parents' house all year long, but in the olive season there was no indulgence or pampering. The basic dish during the harvest was cracked wheat with chickpeas and chicken, along with trays of pastries and pies stuffed with minced meat and onion, buckets of goat's milk, and fresh vegetables picked from a field in the village. Pots of tea simmered on the fire all day long.

The kitchen tasks were not my favourites but there no way to evade them. Ties of kinship did not qualify me for any favourable treatment.

When we were young, we were assigned to pick up the olives that had fallen on the ground or clean the harvested olives of any leaves or dirt. Then, when we were tall enough, we graduated to picking the olives from the tree, each according to his or her height. Later, when we were teenagers and each of us had acquired distinct physical skills or characteristics, the tasks varied. The tallest and most agile were the ones who went up the ladders to pick the olives from the highest branches. In Grandfather's groves, it was forbidden to beat the branches with sticks to bring down the olives, as is done in many groves to speed up the process. Nor did any modern machines ever come into our groves. All the labour was manual, and we deferred to Grandfather's sensitivity towards his trees. He believed that the trees, like us, would be annoyed if they were hit. This would harm our relationship with them and diminish the bounty that flowed to all. The oil would no longer be the best in the world if we mistreated the trees.

Also, as far as we were concerned, speed wasn't important. In fact, on the contrary, speed meant the rituals of the festival would finish early, and that was the last thing we wanted.

When we took a break, we didn't just lie down and drink tea. No, we would play the songs we had chosen carefully throughout the year. These varied from songs popular among young people and songs that the older villagers liked. Then we would start dancing and clapping and cheering as if we were at a real wedding. I would watch the *dabka* dancers form circles and think that the *dabka* was a wonderful example of the joy that can come about only when people act together. If the dancers didn't link arms and didn't move their legs in time with each other, the idea of the *dabka* would completely lose its meaning.

In one of my Spanish lessons, they asked us to talk about folk dances in the countries we came from, and I spoke about the *dabka*; how each part of Syria has its own variant of the dance, with particular music, musical instruments, and traditional costumes, which are different too from the types of *dabka* and of dress in neighbouring countries. I told them that all the stories told in Syria about the origins of the *dabka*, despite their religious, artistic, agricultural and cultural differences, are focused on communal action for the common good.

As usual, Jawan didn't join us in the *dabka* that day. He stood apart, watching us, and leaning against the big family tree. I left the gang and the noise and followed him. He put his arm around my waist for the first time behind the tree. His hand was strong, but his gaze, yes his gaze, was stronger, and that's what stays with me till today.

The short romance that I experienced wasn't the only such romance that began in the olive season. Many first kisses were taken on the sly behind one of those trees. Some of those romances developed and took human shape before our eyes in the form of lovely little babies who joined us at the olive harvest in future seasons, crawling between us and standing to take their first steps among the olive trees, while the pickers clapped and congratulated them.

On one occasion when I slipped away to be alone with Jawan and exchange embraces and quick heated kisses with him, Auntie Umm Sarah spotted us. She was a woman in her seventies, a very close friend of Grandmother's and her right hand in all the preparations for the olive season over the years.

I was in a panic, convinced that she would tell on me to Grandmother, so I prepared myself to face a very embarrassing situation with the family – a situation I didn't yet know how to handle. But Umm Sara looked away from us and pretended to be busy picking up some olives from the ground. She gathered them up in her apron and walked off, humming a gentle sentimental tune as if nothing had happened.

Very well, but we were in a small village and villagers love to share news and rumours. Gossip is one of the most important aspects of life there. That never bothered me because gossip is like the bounty of the soil, shared fairly among everyone.

But even without Umm Sara's intervention I soon noticed that people were gossiping about our amorous adventures. The reports may even have reached my family, though they ignored them, in the belief that this was just a passing phase that any young person might go through. I then realised why some of my friends in the olive gang were avoiding Jawan, especially Salim and those close to him. It was no secret to any of us that Salim had long had special feelings towards me, but there was an unspoken agreement between the members of the gang not to speak out about such things in case it led to a rift in relations between us. This didn't stop the agreement being broken in recent times: after I left, I received news by chance that two friends of mine in the gang had married each other. For a moment I almost felt betrayed because they had kept their relationship secret for years and had maintained it outside the olive season. I was angry that they had been careful to cover it up and felt that they had achieved an undeserved victory over us. But it was just a childish, selfish moment of anger and meant nothing, especially after I left and all the people dispersed in the wake of the war, which I will avoid mentioning as far as is possible.

Umm Sara's own romance stayed with her till her last days. Everyone knew about the wild love affair she had had with the man who finally became her husband. His poverty had threatened their relationship and prevented them from marrying. But eventually Grandmother and the other regular participants in the olive season called a meeting and agreed that part of the proceeds from the next season should go to a special fund for Umm Sara's wedding, from each according to their means. The story is that everyone fulfilled their promises, including the olive trees, which produced more olives than the villagers had ever seen before. Grandmother even wrote 'Love Season' as the headline for that season in the ledger. From then on Umm Sara was the worker most committed to the success of the olive harvest and she often took the lead in setting up solidarity funds to help needy people in the village, without anyone else finding out who they were. She used to say that protecting people's dignity was more important than ensuring they had enough to live on. Maybe that's why she kept my secret.

If I were to give a title to the olive season that brought me together with Jawan, I would just put a full stop – a full stop by which I would wrap up a whole period in my life, a period in which I was very happy. Several olive seasons followed after that and I was eager to take part, although I had already started studying at university in Damascus and it was a long journey by bus to my family's house in the town where they lived and then by car with them to the village. But I hardly remember what happened in those seasons, who was registered in the ledger and who stayed away. During the year I wasn't interested in choosing songs and I didn't know if I would have the energy to clap and mix cheerfully with the others. I would be physically present and go through the motions mechanically, but without emotion. My mind was constantly distracted by the memories that the place evoked in me, as if something deep in my heart had been extinguished, emptying the days of meaning and the future of its appeal.

Grandfather noticed the changes that had come over me in the latter seasons. He didn't ask me any questions or try to put pressure on me, but during one of our last sessions in his office, he turned the globe and pointed at Spain. Then he left on the desk a list of the universities that he had apparently written to and that had accepted me as a post-grad student. All I had to do was confirm that I would go to one of them, and nearby there was a plane ticket. I didn't think about it much. I just said, 'Okay then, let's take a farewell family photo close to the big tree to mark the occasion.'

Emigrating isn't the most difficult thing, David told me a few days ago. Then he kissed me the Syrian way. That's what he called it because it was my way. In fact, I only knew two ways to kiss – Jawan's way and the way other men kiss.

I didn't tell David that, in case it upset him. Despite everything, I haven't become a cruel woman of the kind that hits olive trees with a stick or who can offend a pleasant man. I only told him that I don't think kisses have nationalities and that maybe they're lucky that way. David had a strong desire to come with me on this trip, but I politely dissuaded him because I don't know what I am looking for and I can only find that out when I'm alone. David doesn't think I'm looking for anything, but that doesn't matter because I'm still young and I have enough time to sort out my life.

I met some young men in Damascus and once I almost imagined I had fallen in love with one of them, but visions of Jawan soon came back to wrench my insides.

Like any young woman who has rustic origins and has grown up between the village and a small, marginalised town, I was entranced by Damascus, especially the old part of the city. I could wander around there for hours without getting bored. My favourite parts were those narrow lanes paved with black stone. I loved to look at the extraordinary way the houses fit together. They say that the arched bridges between houses on opposite sides of a street came about because people wanted to extend their houses for when their sons got married, and the only way to do that was to ask their neighbours if they could use their wall as the buttress for a raised extension, or if they would 'lend a shoulder', as the Damascenes put it. Eventually this became a common feature of houses in old parts of the city. Even if this story is imaginary or speculative or more romantic than it should be, the way the houses leaned on the shoulders of other houses struck me as very similar to the way boys and girls lean on each other's shoulders while dancing the *dabka*. I still believe that the idea of a great city such as Damascus has been sustained for thousands of years thanks to this spirit. If that isn't the real story, then the real story must be even more beautiful.

Yesterday I told David I would be in touch with him when I got back to Damascus, then I corrected my slip of the tongue and said, 'Sorry, I mean when I get back to Madrid.' I had a feeling I was confusing this trip on the train from Madrid to the olive groves of Andalusia with that bus trip I used to make from Damascus to the olive groves in the village.

It seems that sometimes you can't leave places, however far away you are, and at other times you don't even need to leave a place in order to travel, like Grandfather and the family tree.

When I moved to Damascus, I rented a studio on the top floor of a building with a view of Mount Qasioun. At first, I was planning to move out into a better apartment because, like most of the old buildings in central Damascus, the building didn't have a lift and the upper floors were exposed to the bad weather in summer and in winter. But what persuaded me to stay in that studio was the cawing of the crows that hovered around it relentlessly. Sometimes I thought they had followed me from the countryside, and they were in Damascus only to carry on looking after me. At other times I tried to work out what they wanted to tell me, because it seemed obvious to me that they insisted on addressing me and I felt there was something urgent they wanted to say. I began reading lots about crows and I thought there might be a way I could learn their language. Once I met an American woman who was studying Arabic in Damascus and she assured me that since she was young, she had noticed that she could speak cat language and that she and the street cats could understand each other perfectly. This made her committed to staying in Damascus longer.

Sometimes when the crow visited me at the break of dawn and cawed close to my window, I could feel the warmth and the taste of Jawan's lips. I felt it was Jawan's breath that misted up the windowpane and that the heart he drew childishly in the condensation with his finger was a real, beating heart. I felt it was Jawan's gaze that hovered around me and in me, and that when the crow flapped its wings it was sending messages that I failed to pick up, like the heart Jawan drew on the windowpane, which turned into drops like tears and then disappeared completely.

In that house in central Damascus, on many days in the month of Ramadan, the woman who lived in the house opposite would leave plates of food outside my door, without asking me my name or whether I was even fasting. I learned from my mother than it was impolite to send the plate back empty, so I would cook something the next day or make a block of *halva* and send a piece back to my neighbour on the plate. Then, the next day, I would get plates of food from the neighbours on the ground floor. So, in that building, where I was a constantly absent-minded student, all the neighbours would be sending each other plates of food, just as they did in the building in the small town where my family lived and where people look out for each other, and in Grandfather's village too of course. Everywhere I lived, plates were passed from house to house, like coded messages with pungent smells, messages of pure love.

Late last year there was an exhibition of photographs by my friend Omar, who lives close to the area where I lived in Damascus. They were photographs of the backstreets of Damascus and the people who live there, as seen by a crow. 'What did that crow make of me when it saw me at the break of dawn?' I thought. 'Did it think I was sad? In love? Beautiful? Abandoned?' But emigration is not the most difficult thing, as David says – David who now looks to me more like that dove that picked up the olive branch in its beak and flew to Noah's Ark. 'Maybe I've started to fall in love with David,' I said, 'or maybe I've started, somehow, to think about surviving.'

While researching the world of crows, I once read that crows don't forget the faces of those who harm them or pose a threat to them. The research says crows teach one another to scold loudly at the dubious face in question, so that a whole community of crows may scold at that same face several years later. In other words, crows in a mob work together to protect the group from danger. In Arabic the word *nafir* is used to describe this kind of communal mobilisation for defence, and naturally the word is associated with war. But as much as possible

I avoid talking about war and its horrors. I run away from it, seal it off and try to ignore it when there is breaking news on the television screen. I don't want to think about the mines that stop people picking the olives or the tree trunks that are now just firewood, the fires that have ravaged the olive groves and drunk the oil straight from the tree trunk, or of the groups of people who set off together to fight other groups of people, or the fate of the plates and their journey between houses, but how can I avoid all that?

I am no longer sure that the sound of the crow I heard in the village on the day Jawan kissed me behind the big tree was really the sound of love. It might have been cawing to warn me of the danger that threatened me, of the danger that was about to kiss me, of the danger that would wreak havoc with my life after he left.

> *The girl with the pretty face*
> *keeps on picking olives*
> *with the grey arm of the wind*
> *wrapped around her waist.*
> *Tree, tree*
> *dry and green.*

Arbolé, arbolé, by Federico Garcia Lorca

The People of North Igra

Anti-capitalist Resistance in the First Half of the 21st Century

Yásnaya Elena Aguilar Gil

Translated from Spanish by Joshua Rackstraw

Prologue: The Story of a Discovery

My first encounter with the Igra people came about by coincidence. Whilst looking through the scant archives that survived the flood of the ancestral territory of the Mixe people during the great climate crisis, I stumbled upon a series of images and documents that caught my eye. Before then, I had barely heard of the Igra people, and to be honest, I wasn't too interested in learning more about the societies of late-stage capitalism.

What else is there to be said about the 20th and 21st centuries? Little can be added to what the historiographical studies have already concluded. The Night of Capitalism, as that era would come to be known, was the time when humanity inexplicably and irrationally opted for the accumulation of wealth over the continued possibility of life. For this accumulation to be possible, the production of (largely unnecessary) goods began on a previously unimaginable scale. The Earth's dwindling natural resources were extracted at such a pace that entire ecosystems were at risk of collapse, and a large part of humankind was put to work in conditions that are now considered abhorrent. The use of fossil fuels – vital to sustain this production – was so intensive that it fundamentally altered the climate of an entire planet, whose temperature rose by three degrees over the span of a few hundred years. The consequences of this are, of course, well known. By 2050, the great climate crisis reached its conclusion, wiping out a large part of humankind in ways which were painful and cruel.

The world that we have reconstructed, over hundreds of years, was developed by the 10% of the population that, despite all odds, survived. There isn't much more to say. Going over the same theories, evidence, and conclusions isn't going to help in our understanding of an ill-fated era which, fortunately, has been consigned to the annals of history. My training, which was carried out within circles of historiographical academics, brought me to the same conclusion.

The People of North Igra

Very little information of interest can be gained from the study of the Night of Capitalism. Current historiography is concerned with the centuries leading up to that time, and deals mostly with the evolving relationship between human societies and various natural ecosystems. The boundaries between Biology, Geography, History, and countless other previously separate disciplines, have become blurred.

My work, carried out in one of the oldest historiographic circles in Mesoamerica, was focused on the study of a race of maize (called *moojk* in the Mixe language) which naturally generates its own fertilisers. It was only thanks to codified knowledge in the oral tradition of the Mixe people that we learned of this plant, as its existence was communicated to us by some of the last speakers of that language. To carry out the research, we got together an interdisciplinary team. My knowledge of the (unfortunately now extinct) Mixe language, and its rich oral tradition, meant I was able to make a reasonable contribution, and I was also experienced with the archives. Our mission was to look for traces of that variety of maize, and for clues as to the possibility that in some part of the Mixe lands, it still grew in the wild. That is to say, in the small part of the territory which isn't now underwater. So many of today's maize crops bear the scars of the chemical and genetic modification carried out during the era of late-stage capitalism, but this variety (if it still exists) could be the key to ensure humankind's continued access to sufficient quantities of food. So as you can see, I was far from interested in the people of North Igra. The efforts of my team were focused elsewhere.

The discovery of the images and documents was therefore incidental to my work. And surprising. Considering everything we knew about the societies of late-stage capitalism, I found it all a little suspect: the photographs and documents dated from the beginning of the 21st Century, but the clothing didn't correspond at all with the fashions of the time. Among the documents, there were schemas; endless lists of names and numbers; documents with exhaustive reports; and what most called my attention, three hand-written bilingual dictionaries; a grammar reference (which was printed by hand, but professionally bound); a diary; and a long series of poems. Upon realising that one of the languages in the texts was Mixe, my surprise reached a whole new level. It was an Igratan-Mixe bilingual dictionary. The words in Mixe were written using the Latin alphabet, adopted at the end of the 20th Century. The Igratan language was also written using Latin in two of the dictionaries, but in the third, it seemed to be codified in characters from the Cherokee syllabary, the famous (and now extinct) language which was spoken in the north of this continent, inside the infamous United States of America, upon which our current writing system is based. That was as much as I could say, based on my linguistic and historical knowledge. Nothing to write home about: I had discovered a few texts related to one of the many languages that were spoken during the Night of Capitalism. From what I knew of the Mixe language, I gathered that the other language was Igratan. Nothing too exciting, to put it bluntly. Similar dead languages had been discovered, at various times in the past.

Given the commitment that I had made with my historiographic circle, it was impossible for me to look into the documents and photos right away. I filed the material away, and I mentioned my discovery to the team, but nobody was that bothered about it. The only thing that caught my eye was the linguistic material: my love for the Mixe language, the language of my ancestors, told me that in these bilingual texts, new aspects of Mixe could be revealed by the light of the Igratan language. Mere curiosity. Simple linguistic fun. After sharing my reports on the *moojk* variety of maize with the team for evaluation, I decided to take a few days off in my homeland. Before leaving, I told the others of my intention to take the material I had discovered with me, which they were okay with, or at least, indifferent to. Trise Ayoop, a young researcher who had recently joined the Circle of Historiography, made a slightly unsettling comment before leaving: 'I've always had the feeling that not everything was as homogenous as they say during the Night of Capitalism, I hope you find some refreshing ideas in those papers.' Words that turned out to be quite prophetic.

Once I got to my village, I dedicated my days to my community obligations, and at night, I got to work on the documents I had brought with me. My first task was to use my knowledge of Mixe to decode the Igratan language, which took no more than eight weeks. After that, I was ready to read the rest of the material. These texts would, of course, come to radically change my idea of the Night of Capitalism. But at that time, I went back to the historiographic circle completely unaware of the new world that awaited me.

Coming back to my duties as part of the research team, I totally forgot about the Igra texts. It wasn't until eight weeks later when, whilst off work recovering from a seasonal flu, I went back to look at the material. Little by little, I discovered that I was reading part of the communal archives of an Igra village which had established links with two Mixe communities from that time. What I managed to understand from the contents of the documents, and from the images, led me to believe that the commonly-held idea that absolutely all sociopolitical life at the beginning of the 21st century was regulated by the structure of nation-states was false. The more I read, the more I was convinced that I should share these ideas with my colleague Trise Ayoop. Thanks to her enthusiasm and persistence, we were able to convince our team to fully commit to the investigation of these texts, and to the search for further evidence. We were able to explore the archives, do some travelling, and look for a coherent narrative based on the artefacts that were uncovered as a result of our efforts. Over the last four years, I'm happy to say that many have aided us in our research, as it is important to do historical justice to all the peoples, communities and socio-political structures that rebelled against the Night of Capitalism. This is especially true for those who would otherwise be forgotten.

The current understanding is that our society, economics, and relationship with nature were all established after the great climate crisis. But our research would suggest that this is not the case. It seems that in the deepest darkness of the Night of Capitalism, there were small nations that fought against the tide with practices that were ideologically opposed to capitalism. Many of these nations, such as the people of North Igra, did not survive the ravages of the climate crisis, but we are certain that these practices have somehow pulled through, perhaps through a collective memory that, like an underground river, flowed through the crisis and emerged as a bubbling spring in the societies that we have built today. So desperate are we to distance ourselves from the Night of Capitalism that we have, to our shame, forgotten the cultures that pursued sustainable life in the midst of a time when death reigned. Regrettably, the righteous and justified condemnation of late capitalism has blinded us to the fact that, despite the horrendous conditions of the time, there were communities and peoples that fought back. We believe it fair that they are recognised as the precursors of a new world, the world that we now inhabit. Little by little, we must banish the idea that all of humanity was under the yoke of capitalism. No longer can we use the term 21st century society as shorthand for capitalism, aware as we are that not all humanity bought into the culture of destruction. It seems that the all-consuming nature of capitalism, and the once-popular myth that it was the only possible way to exist, has tricked us into believing it was a pandemic, a totalitarian regime which was impossible to escape. We are now able to prove that this was not the case. Although the efforts of these communities and peoples failed to stop the great climate crisis that almost wiped out humanity, their resistance, their vision of how nature should heal, survived to the present day. The world that we have made for ourselves already existed in the minds of the people that tried to warn the hegemonic capitalist societies of the imminent apocalypse. We are lucky to be able to reap the fruits of the seed they planted long ago, and we should not allow our pride and our forgetful nature to blind us to the fact that the roots of our societies go deep.

As we continue to investigate, we find more and more evidence that peoples such as the Mixe and the Igra, even in the golden age of capitalism, held onto practices and knowledge that went against the prevailing tide which, we now know, was pulling humanity towards the brink of destruction. What follows is a brief description of the principles that guided North Igra culture in connection with other communities in resistance in the midst of the Night of Capitalism, just decades before the climate crisis. There are three sections: *Lands and Territories; Government*, and *Festivals*. The documents and evidence that we have found over several years of interdisciplinary research are fragments that only make sense if they are considered within their context. Previous publications have already been made including technical details of artefacts, documents, and images related to the people of North Igra (and their relationships with other communities); due to the enthusiasm with which this work was received, we have created this report, which is suitable for non-academic readers. It includes conclusions drawn from several years of findings, reconstructions created from scraps of documents, images, and other objects from the period. It is not exhaustive, rather, we have focused on pieces that reveal the overwhelming narrative of the Igra people as an island of resistance in a sea of capitalism. The text also includes comparisons between features of capitalist societies from that era, and practices which are now common. Now that we are aware of the existence of these small pockets of resistance, and the contact between the Igra people and other communities working outside the capitalist system, further research is needed in order to fully reveal the extent to which these communities were working together. I would like to thank the historiographic circles that made this work possible, as well as the researchers, publishers, educational teams, worker's collectives, and all those who have supported us for so long. Without their tireless efforts, this report would not exist.

Yasnaya Elena A. Gil

I. Notes on the People of North Igra

Let's start with an idea which has long been considered fact: throughout the 20th and 21st centuries, all human societies were capitalist. Some researchers have suggested that this system was so all-consuming and totalitarian that it controlled the lives, desires and imaginations of even the smallest villages and tribes, far from the urban metropolises. It has been asserted, time and again, that the idea that well-being and progress were inextricably linked to capitalism was universally accepted as fact. This limited and unimaginative concept is revealed as erroneous when we consider the people of North Igra, who were once found in the area which was known as Mesoamerica.

Their name suggests that there was once a South Igra, but so far, no evidence has been found demonstrating this to be true. The Igra communities shared borders with the Mixe people, to the south; the Otomangues, to the west; and the Michiko people, to the north. Their proximity to the ocean explains their disappearance, due to the flooding caused by rising ocean levels in the second half of the 21st century. We can estimate, based on evidence from the era, that the population of the region oscillated between 130,000 and 150,000 people. The main activities in the region were farming, hunting, and, of course, fishing. Due to the geographical peculiarities of their area, the Igra territory was incredibly diverse, and was in fact made up of several different ecosystems, with coniferous pine and oak forests in the west, a small desert in the north, jungles in the south, and a warm coastal region in the east. Our research supports the hypothesis that this diversity goes some way in explaining the complex relationship that the Igra people have with the notion of land and territory (for more detail, see the part of this report entitled *Management of Lands and Territories*).

There is no evidence that the Igratan language was related to any of the known languages of the region. Further research may be needed to see what links, if any, can be established. We do not know much about the evolution of Igra literacy, only that they used two different orthographic systems: at the time from which the evidence dates (the first half of the 21st century) they mostly used the Latin alphabet, but older texts are written in the ancient syllabary of the Cherokee people, the same one that has inspired the graphic system with which we now write this report. Our analysis indicates that the Cherokee syllabary was used for poetic and ritualistic texts, while the Latin script was used for other activities that involved writing. This can be explained by the fact that the Latin alphabet, by the 21st century, had become the orthographic system preferred by the capitalist system. Just as we now use, for almost all purposes, a contemporary version of the old Cherokee syllabary, during the Night of Capitalism, orthographic systems with a more phonological cut were preferred over the diverse writing systems coming from other cultures, many of which have not survived to this day. How did the Igra come to adopt the Cherokee syllabary, which was developed thousands of kilometres to the north? This question is still a mystery, and could be the subject of future research. We must not, however, allow our interest in linguistic matters to distract us from the more important lessons that the Igra people can teach us.

II. The People of North Igra and the *Tunjënpet*

The revelation that North Igra society was based on a concept diametrically opposed to the ideology that emerged from capitalism at the time is, of course, at the core of this report. This mindset explains the functioning of the economy, its government, its system of justice, and its relationship with the land. In the Igra language, this idea is called *tunjënpet*, which can be roughly translated as profound reciprocity. Within the bilingual dictionary whose discovery was key to this investigation, it is stated that the Mixe translation for this term would be *kumunytunk*. It would appear that for the Mixe people too, profound reciprocity was a guiding principle for social affairs; an idea which we had long suspected.

Who would have thought that in the midst of the Night of Capitalism, in its late stage, there were societies whose functioning was based on the notion of profound reciprocity? All evidence indicates that these small communities were organised differently from the hegemonic societies of the time. Just as the idea of reciprocity is at the foundation of today's societies, it was also the guiding mindset for this small network of communities and, it would appear, for several neighbouring villages.

Before we continue, it's important to establish some differences between the notion of profound reciprocity which we have today and the *tunjënpet* of the People of North Igra at the beginning of the 21st century. Although they would seem to refer to the same principle, there are some important differences. For today's societies, profound reciprocity orders sociopolitical relations through communal principles that we learn from childhood; for the Igra people, the notion of *tunjënpet* was a sacred principle which was not usually discussed openly, despite being at the heart of daily life, and despite the fact that this principle flew in the face of the dominant ideological and economic ideas of the time. It would not be inaccurate to say that the concept of reciprocity, as we currently understand it, is institutionalised. For the Igra people, it was ritualistic. In today's societies, the notion of profound reciprocity is the subject of studies, stories, art; it is an issue for public debate; just as democracy was a fundamental concept for the nation-states of late capitalism, profound reciprocity is widely recognised as being at the heart of the ideology that underpins our world today. For the Igra communities, in the midst of the Night of Capitalism, this was not the case. It is possible that the pressure exerted by the capitalist nation-states, and their noisy idea of progress, meant that the sentimental notion of reciprocity was banished to the realm of the sacred. To the capitalist philosophy of the time, *tunjënpet* must have been akin to an almost quasi-mystical belief system, and not, therefore, a viable and fundamental concept on which it would be possible to base a political system, or a society. As it was not considered a threat to the status quo, the concept of deep reciprocity guaranteed its continued existence. Evidence of *tunjënpet* can be found in many cultural and political aspects of the lives of the Igra people. *Tunjënpet* was not only at the core of human interaction; it was also a vital part of the relationship held with the forces of nature. The structure of the Igra government was also mediated by this notion, as well as the way in which festivals were organised and held.

III. Lands and Territories

Unlike the capitalist notion of the earth as a provider of natural resources to be exploited for economic gain, the Igra people viewed humanity as simply another element that made up the land. The idea of humanity in opposition to nature was not part of the Igra worldview. To better explain this, we propose a possible scale that explains the ways in which humanity has coexisted with the land and its ecosystems, and then locate the Igra notion of territory on this scale.

On one end of the scale, we can find nomadic societies that neither own nor belong to the land, that travel the face of the earth according to its changing seasons to ensure access to food. These societies' notion of territory comes from their constant movement. During the winter, they move to warmer lands, and during summer, they seek cool weather. Though few of these societies exist, these days there are communities like the Dresderian people, whose nomadic lifestyle follows the rhythm of the seasons. They have little or no concept of land ownership, rather, they live in a state of constant flux.

On the next point of this scale, we find sedentary societies that, while they do not have a formalised system of land ownership, see the earth as a mother; a provider of food and a sustainer of life, including human life, among other ecosystems. It's interesting that the role of mother is often given to the earth, and the role of father goes to the sun, who fertilises. The notion of territory of these societies is based on agriculture, and the effect of the seasons on farming, planting, harvesting, etc. The present-day nation of Catepoza is one example of this type of society.

Further on the scale lie sedentary societies with a developed and complex notion of communal land ownership. The majority of present-day communities work in this way, although the limits of communal, rather than private, ownership are not as absolute as those borders between capitalist nation-states of the past. There is an awareness of the borders in the public imagination, but also an awareness that they are porous, so to speak. They give identity to the peoples of the world. In this type of society, the notion of territory comes from collective ownership.

And finally, at the far end of the scale, we find capitalist societies with a complex notion of territory based on the idea of private, individual ownership. As absurd as it may seem to us now, in capitalist societies it was possible for a person to own a part of the face of the earth, despite the fact that it was not a product, nor was it the result of a manufacturing process. According to this logic, if you owned a portion of land, you were free to exploit the natural resources that the land provided. What's more, the size and borders of the territories owned by individuals were totally arbitrary, ignoring all naturally occurring boundaries, and were assigned via a legal document called a property deed. As if this situation were not bizarre enough, it was also possible to buy, rent, or sell portions of the face of the earth in exchange for money. The same was true with natural assets such as water and, eventually, air. In this type of society, the notion of territory is generated from treating the land as a commodity that can be bought or sold on the market. Fortunately, this absurd mindset no longer exists in contemporary society.

So, where on the scale can we place the communities of the people of North Igra? The evidence suggests that, to our great surprise, the Igra communities, in the midst of the Night of Capitalism, had two different notions of territory that were totally unrelated to the idea of land as property: on the one hand, there were fishing and mountain communities that considered land as collective property, with this collective property delimited in the imagination through traditional songs and narratives that passed from generation to generation. In the collective consciousness, these narratives became a symbolic extension of their territory, whose limits never became borders. The Igra communities of the desert were, on the other hand, semi-nomadic, and would move to warmer climes in the winter. Their notion of territory was created step by step in their movements throughout the year.

For each of the Igra communities, the link between humanity and nature was established and mediated via *tunjënpet*. The relationship was formalised through a series of rituals that established a correspondence with the provider ecosystems, and with the other entities that inhabited them. Given that the Igra population would have to take the life of certain animals and plants in order to feed the community, it was necessary that communal work be carried out three times a year. This work, done in the spirit of the common good and in order to establish an equal relationship with the forces of nature and the other entities that populated the ecosystems, was called *tequio* (it seems that this word is a late loan, but we still do not have enough evidence to conclusively prove this to be true).

This *tequio*, involving poetic, musical and ritual offerings, was held for three days and was organised by specialists. The *tequio* was, therefore, the collective manifestation of profound reciprocity with the earth and its forces. Families would carry out ceremonies of reciprocity with the land whenever they deemed it convenient, but the collective *tequio* offering was carried out three times a year. From the capitalist viewpoint, these rituals were merely an ethnographic oddity, rather than a manifestation of a radically different notion of territory, and a novel way of interacting with nature (to be precise, 'nature' is not a good translation; all available evidence suggests that the Igratan word *yää* means 'all that is' or 'everything that exists', so it does not imply the marked difference between nature and humanity which is typical of capitalist discourse). This type of *tequio* regulated the very heart of the notion of territory for the Igra communities, if the land sustained and fed the Igra people, the Igra people manifested collective reciprocity in the form of ritual. The details of these *tequio* rituals are not very clear, we believe that the little evidence we found has to do with their sacred nature.

IV. System of Government

The system of government of the Igra communities was also permeated by the notion of profound reciprocity and, therefore, had *tequio* at its heart. It is possible to consider the structure of the government itself as the manifestation of a sustained but rotating *tequio*. To begin with, it is important to note that the Igra people did not have any central government; each of the communities (it is not clear how many communities there were, although we have counted at least twenty) had an assembly as the highest governing body, and the assembly of one community had no power over the affairs of other Igra communities. Although different communities would often work together, the Igra people never tried to centralise power in a singular government body. The Igra communities found an interesting way to apparently comply with the demands of the nation-state while maintaining their own political structures: while official reports were created indicating that the elections in each community had been carried out according to state regulations, the local government was actually chosen in a different way: each year, community members over the age of 18 would choose who would form the new government. The rotation of people within the system of self-government was important to ensure the integration of all people, avoiding the creation of a political class. Participation in local government was not financially compensated, but carried a certain social prestige: members of the government were carrying out a collective, year-long *tequio*, sacrificing their own time and effort for the collective good. Since participating in local government was not compensated, and due to the constant scrutiny that governors experienced from the electorate, people would argue against being elected at each election assembly. Unlike the parties of the capitalist nation-state of the time, the people who made up the local government for a period did not actively seek political power. In fact, they would attempt to provide reasons as to why they were unsuitable for election. We might consider the local government of each Igra community (nomadic or sedentary) as more of a coordinating body that carried out the wishes of the assembly. In this way, in the midst of the Night of Capitalism, the Igra communities maintained a *tequio*-government that opposed the logic of the nation-state.

Unremunerated community service (i.e., *tequio*) was a fundamental mechanism for the achievement of the goals of the community. If the desire of an Igra community was to build a bridge, as documented in one case in the archives, the members of the local government coordinated the *tequio*, which also included the sourcing of the raw material. When necessary, economic contributions were made for materials that had to be acquired in the external capitalist market. *Tequio* was also the first response in case of emergency. We found evidence of a flood which occurred at the beginning of the climate crisis, after which the Igra communities organised a two-week *tequio* with the aim of rescuing as many people as possible, and building a new village. When the mechanisms put in place by the state were unable to cope with the scale and the speed of the floods, *tequio* was there to meet the needs of the people. The Igra government system itself came about as the result of a collective *tequio* that, in turn, executed *tequios* to satisfy collective desires, meet the community's needs, and respond to emergencies. *Tequio* was the social technology *par excellence* for the Igra culture. All the evidence we have found so far leads us to believe that the system of self-government of the Igra communities is, in fact, surprisingly similar to the functioning of our own communities, with some differences that we detail below.

The fact that the Igra people were able to maintain these social and political practices is even more surprising considering that they did so during the Night of Capitalism, and the natural disasters that heralded the beginning of the great climate crisis. Their way of life and, in particular, *tequio*, was not exempt from the influences and pressures exerted by capitalism and they did, when necessary, interact with the market and the state. In fact, in one of the documents discovered by the team, one can read the lament of an old woman who, in the form of a song, complains that young people are shirking the practices of their elders and that, literally, 'they no longer donate their hand nor sweat to their people.' This verse strongly suggests the idea of *tequio* although, as we have noted, the term was not referred to directly at the time. Unlike the current situation, the system of government and the *tequio* were not ideologically hegemonic mechanisms as is the case with profound reciprocity today, which, without pressure of any kind, has become the basis of balance. It is, without doubt, an incredible achievement that the Igra people maintained their practices even in the face of the overwhelming might of the forces of capitalism that reigned at that time. That their resistance disappeared in the floods, caused by the great climate crisis that wiped their territories from the map, is a tragedy.

V. Festival as a form of *tequio*

In this section, we briefly describe the notion of the festival as another manifestation of *tunjënpet*. Festivals seem to have been a fundamental element of resistance, although unfortunately we have found little documentation detailing the way in which festivals were held, or even how often they took place. But despite the lack of details, the archives show that the collective festivals of the Ingra people were fundamental as mechanisms of opposition to capitalism. Each party could be considered as a *tequio* in itself, an enjoyment-oriented *tequio* with little intervention of money or market logic. While festivals within the capitalist system were used to demonstrate the wealth and power of those who organised them, the Igra population used them as a mechanism for distributing wealth for collective enjoyment. The farmers that had enjoyed a better harvest, or the fishing communities who had pulled a more bountiful haul, provided the food. Those who were not able to provide food, provided work, creativity, music or dance. Each contribution was celebrated equally; the fact that a family could not contribute grain, for example, did not result in a loss of social prestige; their contribution of music was considered as important as the food to allow the party to take place. The festivities, oriented towards enjoyment, were also a chance to release social tensions and conflicts derived from the intense debates in the political assemblies. For each party, a committee was formed to carry out the duties and responsibilities involved in the party planning, with members of the community taking turns to help out. Festivals were conceived, and also held, as *tequio*. There is evidence of family parties in which profound reciprocity also prevailed, and in which gifts and work were exchanged. If one family helped another in the planning and execution of a party, the latter would, at a later date, return the favour. We can therefore conclude that festivals were an important social element in which the principle of profound reciprocity was exercised.

VI. Conclusion

As we have seen, at the beginning of the 21st century, the communities of the Igra people had *tunjënpet* at the heart of their families and their social life, something similar to what we now call profound reciprocity. In opposition to the dominant trends of the time, these minuscule social structures flew in the face of the hegemonic system, and functioned with a logic that was quite the opposite of late capitalism. The pressure placed on these communities from the macrosystem in which they existed meant that their practices were at constant risk. The principle of *tunjënpet* manifested itself as *tequio* and also as mutual support between individuals and families. The value given to reciprocity manifested itself through *tequio*: ritual *tequio* was used to give back to the land and its ecosystems, *tequio* was used to establish relationships between people and the community to which they belonged, and *tequio* was used to organise and carry out festivities. Before these findings were published, the complexity, scale, and depth of these anti-capitalist practices, carried out at a time when capitalism seemed inescapable, had never been fully understood. We believe it is fair that these once-forgotten people be recognised and given justice, since in the course of our research we found evidence of this same type of practice in other regions of our continent, codified in other languages, using other names. Our research indicates that the practice of profound reciprocity was commonplace not only for the Igra people, but for other communities and peoples. Alongside some aspects of the Igra economic system that are not yet fully understood, further research is needed to get an accurate idea of how far these practices spread.

The system of profound reciprocity which orders and rules our world did not burst, fully formed, into existence after the climate crisis. It grew, in fact, from a seed planted during the irrational rat race of capitalism, at a time when it seemed humanity was destined to destroy itself. The Igra people planted that seed.

Summer, 2275.

The People of North Igra: Anti-capitalist Resistance in the First Half of the 21st Century Network of historiography collectives.

Co-ordinated by:
Abi, Solei
Ayoop, Trise
Dollarga, Julio
Ene, Adi
Gil, Yasnaya Elena A.
Gondra, Gus
Juun, Gader
Mito, Mejy
Meles, Luste
Nanto, Indira
Questre, Yanda
Trizbea, Xëë
Yoots, Granter

Ukuza kukaNxele
Or,
Time Passes

Panashe Chigumadzi

Sth,

the Time is now.

Mayibuye, iAfrika!

Sth, it has been done. The fire is lit. Crowds gather around.

Mayibuye, iAfrika!

Sth, the tension and release we feel as we watch the flames lick the stump of Rhodes' statue. Our hearts beat fast in exhilaration. With our matchsticks we are liberating this country!

Mayibuye, iAfrika!

Sth, books, and paintings reduced to ashes. A 1652 screams in horror: 'The fire of the Roman legions invading Egypt, devouring the papyrus scrolls of the Library of Alexandria!' A 2000 BC x 200 AD screams in delight: 'Bulawayo burning!'

Mayibuye, iAfrika!

Oya! Ogun! Shango! Be with us!

Mayibuye, iAfrika!

Sth, flames restore personhood to things.

Mayibuye, iAfrika!

Sth, this night's fire will cleanse the souls of The Wretched. Cleanse Baas of his Baaskap. Cleanse Boys and Girls of their Boy-and-Girl-hood.

Mayibuye, iAfrika!

Things we lost in the fire: the myth that we will always lose. Things we gained in the fire: the knowledge that we can win.

Mayibuye, iAfrika!

Sth, as Azania burns closer and closer, sweat beads form on foreheads of us crazy Comrades. Are we high on the smoke fumes? Or are we high on hallucinations of Azania?

Mayibuye, iAfrika!

Sth, Comrades pour out a lil' liquor for amadlozi we no longer have the words to communicate with for having mastered the tongue of master. Libations for all the revolutionaries, who in their short lives, set fire to the world. And quickly burnt through their own spirits only to combust in a huff of smoke.

Mayibuye, iAfrika!

Sth, the police come in, swiftly surround you. Are you shot because you are Black?

Are you Black because you are shot?

Welcome Black.

Welcome Black.

Welcome Black.

Mayibuye, iAfrika?

Sth, you resist, and they overpower you. Three police vans worth of students and workers shoved inside.

Mayibuye, iAfrika?

The police van starts with a jerk and then picks up speed. Your bodies bang and hit the sides like loose bottles.

Let us out! Stop! Some shout. Some sing. Some cry. Some bang on windows. Some have presence of mind, take out their phones, upload:

#PoliceBrutality
#PoliceIntimidation
#MaxPrice4BlackLife
#RhodesMustFall

Mayibuye, iAfrika?
You are quiet until you get there.
Mayibuye, iAfrika?
A stocky 1652 policeman looking like apartheid, pulls you out. Some try to dispose of bags with rocks. The 1652 policeman catches you, 'You think you are clever, hey? I will teach you a lesson.'
Mayibuye, iAfrika?
Comrades singing outside the station.
Mayibuye, iAfrika?
Your lawyers are here. You'll be out on bail soon; they just need to process you all. It won't be long. They've assured you.
Mayibuye, iAfrika?
It's now dark. Comrades are still singing outside the station.
Mayibuye, iAfrika?
There is no singing anymore. Comrades have had to go home.
Mayibuye, iAfrika?
'Yhu, hayi,' Comrade Bae throws his hands up and walks away from the remaining lawyer. Brenda Marechera pulls out a bottle of snuff, sneezes as you watch her. Seeing your expectant face, she picks up your chin,
   'Silinde ukuza kukaNxele.'

8 February 2016. 20h15.
'Silinde ukuza kukaNxele.'
Brenda repeats this to you as the warden locks the gates behind you and the 15 other Comrades in your cell.

In your holding cell, you keep inside the courtyard and don't go into the enclosure with the steel toilet. The cinderblock wall beside it has long fingerlike streaks of shit. Not that it's any better outside. The blankets and mattresses the officers instructed us to fetch also smell like shit. You'd rather shiver.

8 February 2016. 22:27.

As you shuffle around with your shitty blankets and mattresses, Brenda Marechera suddenly gets up, 'Gio-gio!'

You all stand up to attention, 'Gio!'

'Gio-gio!'

From down the corridor, you hear the voice of Comrade Bae, joining your chorus, 'Gio!'

'Gio-gio!'

'Gio!'

A full chorus now.

'Gio-gio!'

'Gio!'

'Gio-mama-gio!'

'Gio!'

'Gio-ma-guerilla!'

'Gio!'

'Gio-gio-gio'

'Gio!'

'Pamberi ne Chimurenga, pamberi!'

'Pamberi!'

'Pamberi ne hondo, pamberi!'

'Pamberi!'

'From Cape to Cairo
  From Morocco to Madagascar
         Azania
        Azania
      Azania
     Azania
    Azania

        Azania
Azania
   Azania
      Azania
         Azania
           Azania
              Azania
                 Azania
                    Azania
                 Azania
             Azania
          Azania
     From Cape to Cairo
 From Morocco to Madagascar
          Azania
        Azania
     Azania
Azania
   Azania
     Azania
       Azania
         Azania
            Azania
              Azania
           Azania
         Azania
       Azania
     Azania
   Azania
Azania

                    Azania
                            From Cape to Cairo
                                    From   Morocco   to
Madagascar
                            Azania
                    Azania
            Azania

8 February 2016. 23:04.
The guards, enough of you after what feels like hours, order you to be quiet.
You dance in silence,
to the memory of the Rhythm,
the rhythm of Struggle.
If the Song stopped playing, would you survive the silence?
Who knows where Our Time goes?
For the answer to that I'm afraid we'll wait, ukuza kukaNxele.

Time Passes

Ukuza kukaNxele Or, Time Passes

Who knows what Time is?

We think uNxele might say, more than chronology, more than the medium through which we pass, measured in the experience of the quotidian and extraordinary. Time separates heartbeats from deaths, questions from answers, sorrows from laughters, hates from loves, oppressions from freedoms. Time separates heartbeats from heartbeats, deaths from deaths, questions from questions, answers from answers, sorrows from sorrows, laughters from laughters, hates from hates, loves from loves, oppressions from oppressions, freedoms from freedoms. Time makes breathtaking, impersonal swoops; seasons through years through decades through centuries through millennia. Time is elastic: changes, slow to release themselves in the burst of long-held tensions. It is of fluid rhythm and pace, the speed of light, the geological slow of stalactite forming. Time is the temperamental conductor of our lives, choosing its own tempo and force. At Times, it is not linear, making unexpected leaps forwards and backwards. It transcends its own forward tick. minute, second, hour, suspended, allowing us momentarily to forget about Time. Time, the medium through which we live, even as we forget the oppression of its ominous tick.

Who knows where Our Time goes?

For the answer to that I'm afraid we'll wait, silinde ukuza kukaNxele.

Time Passes

Who knows where Our Time goes?

It must go to whom it belongs. The old gods of Time cry, Our Time no longer answers to us. Our Time obeys Baas. Give or take, 500 years, Time has been under new management. The new gods of Time attempt to reign its tempo and force, dictate its rhythm and pace. In their hands Time becomes malleable, oppressive. The new gods of Time are capricious and even more temperamental. At Times, speeding our clocks along, spinning Time's hands into a blur, other Times the new gods might stop them entirely to dwell on a suspended moment. Under the new gods, Our Time arrives and departs unpredictably with our lives. This is the power of a god. The old gods of Time cry, Our Time no longer answers to us. Our Time obeys Baas. Our Time now functions according to rules it has never known, at least not until the new gods crossed the seas. To signify our disrespect of Time, they call it African Time. But pray, tell, how can we respect Time if we no longer own it? How do we respect Time if it no longer serves us?

Who knows where Our Time goes?

For the answer to that I'm afraid we'll wait, silinde ukuza kukaNxele.

Time Passes

1816.

uNxele, our prophet, sees into the Past, the beginning of the rupture of Time. It begins, uNxele says, when Thixo, the god of the new gods of Time, clashed with Mdalidiphu, Creator of the Deep, the god of the old gods of Time. The new gods of time, uNxele says, murdered the son of their god. Angry, heartbroken, Thixo expelled the new gods of time from their land into the water, which, treacherous, brought the new gods of Time to our land to dispossess us of Our Time. Alas, uNxele says, Mdalidiphu is a powerful god. Mdalidiphu will, In Time, help his gods reclaim Their Time. The old gods of time, uNxele advises, must worship Mdalidiphu, dancing, enjoying life, making love so that their progeny would increase and fill the world. Hearing this, the old gods of Time cry in despair, how long must we wait until Mdalidiphu defeats Thixo? uNxele remains silent. The old gods of Time continue to cry, when Mdalidiphu eventually defeats Thixo will we have any Time left?

Who knows where Our Time goes?

Silinde ukuza kukaNxele.

Time Passes

26 June 1860.
The iron bull charges forward.
The iron bull's bell-ow rings throughout Earth's ears, announcing a new murderous time. Wake up! A second, low drawn-out blast from the locomotive horn disperses the last remnants of sleep. A third—louder, nearer—pounding in our hearts.

The iron bull's bell-ow reaches our confused spirits. 'Vuka, vuka, sekusile!' uMandubulu, the large black owl, helper of our ancestors, used to call. *Wake up, wake up,* it has dawned. 'Woza la! Si lapha,' the cock, helper of our ancestors, used to crow. *Come over here! This is where we are!*

The iron bull's bell-ow rings through our spirits, and a terrifying sense echoes deep down in our being: This is no longer where we are. Where are our ancestors? Where are our descendants? Where are we? When are we?

(We are) Too late.
(We are) Out of time.

The iron bull's bellow has taken over the cock's crow. *Wake up!* There is no dawn, only deep night. *Come over here! This inferno is where we are!* The iron bull charges forward, yoking us flesh beasts of burden to modernity's march of progress. A gun rings. A sjambok cracks. This iron bull, the iron carriage of time conscripts us. Lamps flicker. A thin sharp whistle. This iron cage of time locks us in and shoots us down,

deepdeepdeepdeepdeepdown to where they are: Hell.
The iron bull charges forward.
The iron cage slows down. It stops. Out of the mine, boys jump.

Time Passes

8 February 2016. 12h18.
'Amandla Comrades.'
'Amandla!'
Brenda stills the room and makes way for another Comrade. You recognize him with this Amilcar Cabral looking beret from twitter as Comrade Bae.

You are late. Brenda stands at attention next to a Comrade addressing the group of Comrades gathered outside Azania House.

'Amandla Comrades.'
'Amandla!'
'We cannot tolerate this situation Comrades. It is unacceptable. One week of the academic year has already passed and they've still failed to resolve the accommodation issue. They gave us temporary accommodation with the promise that they would resolve it by the end of the week. Last they came with that resolution of theirs: we received communication that we have by the end of the weekend to vacate and go back home.'

'With what money? Asinamli!'
'Vele, Asinamali'
'Amandla Comrades.'
'Amandla!'
'Comrades, when they decided to demolish Barnato Residence to make way for parking, we warned them that accommodation would be an issue. They ignored us because they know their own children live in the suburbs and they were only concerned with where they can park their expensive cars bought with stolen money!'

'Izwe!'
'How many meetings, Comrades? How many letters? How many occupations? How many times have we tried to negotiate with them? Your guess is as good as mine Comrades.'
'Buwa!'
'Comrades, it seems they cannot understand us Natives when we beg and plead and cry, even if it's this English of theirs. What language must we use?'
'Buwa!'
'Comrades, we have tried to speak nicely, even in this English of theirs, but we have seen that Baas has simply closed his ears, evicted us, and told us Natives to go back to our townships and bantustans!'
'Izwe!'
'Comrades, the time for talking is over.'
'Izwe Lethu!'
'Comrades, they have given us no choice, we are going to have to take matters into our own hands. We must reclaim Azania! Amandla Comrades!'
'Amandla!'
'Mayibuye!'
'iAfrika!'
'Mayibuye!'
'iAfrika!'
'Mayibuye!'
'iAfrika!'

Time Passes

Ukuza kukaNxele Or, Time Passes

21 August 1791.

Cecile Fatiman, high priestess of Voudun calls on the ancestors and commands their descendants: rise up against the new gods of Time! Her people's Time, almost 200 years had built Saint Dominigue, exporter of 60% of the world's coffee and 40% of the world's sugar. Led by Touissant Louvetre, they fight for their Time. They defeat Napolean's people. It seems the old gods of Time are free! They are the gods of Time once more! In all of the Atlantic so singular is this defeat, can any other achieve it? At what cost?

Time Passes

8 February 2016. 20:39.
You are grateful for the presence of the other Comrades. You don't know how you were going survive this shit alone. In central booking, the officers had wanted to put you all into individual cells. This, after your Comrades objected to group cell allocation according to gender, well sex as you'd pointed out, but the officers didn't want to hear it. They were just doing their jobs, which didn't include this Decolonisation What What of you spoilt Model C kids running around starting fires because you are Ungrateful. Protest yes, it's a Noble Cause we understand, but why must you burn? Especially the libraries, in Our Time we were disciplined. Just because we go to that university does not mean we are all Model C! Some of us live in the same community as you! And where were you when we were protesting peacefully! We are doing this for your children! Whatever. When they eventually suggested the single cells, you capitulated and agreed to the colonial gender-sex binary for fear of your safety.

Time Passes

7 September 1978. 23:05.

Sindisiwe is now Late, her Time has come. It is a Sunday; we wait to bury her next Saturday. An UnTimely Death, Baas had said. Yes, she was still Mama's baby. Baas didn't hear her, he continued, You People die like flies. You will bury her on the weekend, not on My Time. She cries, will I ever bury on My Time?

Time Passes

8 February 2016. 20:45.
'He was going to kill me, so I stabbed him. The officer arrested us both when I reported it,' says the woman another woman with whom the sixteen of you are sharing a cell. Dishevelled, she looks in her early twenties.

Time Passes

4 June 1994.

An old woman stands wary in a queue, her great grandchild holding her, supporting her weight. The new Department of Home Affairs is issuing new papers that bring people into Time. Impatient, the official asks the mama again what year she was born in.

'Abazali bam bathi ndazalwa ngomnyaka weenkumbi,' she says.

The official asks, impatient again, 'Heh, the year of the Caterpillar?'

'Yes', the woman responds, 'Andinalwazi ncam ngoba sasithiywa ngokweziganeko, kodwa kuthwa sisganeko esehla kufuphi kunemfazwe yehlabathi yokuqala.'

'You are telling me this year of the caterpillar could have been before World War One?' Is it not mind boggling that she couples the occurrence with white men's foolishness?

This was why she was wary, she foresaw this trouble, that they would not understand her Time. She did try to explain that in their time, children and years were named after Iziganeko, the system of Amaqaba, the unconverted. But they didn't have time to listen to this strange way of doing things. So, 1 January 1908 they gave her.

Time Passes

December 1971.
Western region, Nigeria. The man died.

Time Passes

April 1970.

Pretoria Central Prison. Prisoner 1323/69 makes a decision. She will not take solitary confinement anymore. She will spare her comrades the pain of continued confinement. Revolutionary suicide. No better method of focusing the world's attention on the terror of the Terrorism Act.

She had already made another decision, when Tata was arrested: 'I will fight them to the last drop of my blood. I am going to fight them, and I am not going to let them break me. I will never let them break me. I am going to be who my father taught me to be. They will know me by name: Zanyiwe Madikizela.'

Time Passes

3 March 2013. 05:01.

Lerato is almost hit by a group of cyclists. She doesn't see that she's in the bicycle lane. She's rushing for the Metrobus queue. The other commuters are already standing drearily with an air of defeat waiting over them. Transport queues on Monday mornings are an anti-climax after the weekend's excesses. Lerato comes along panting. Somebody in the queue asks when the bus will ever be On Time?

Time Passes

1950-something.

Achebe sits at his desk, feverish with the desire, a familiar one, to recover the Time of the old gods from the darkness the new gods have relegated it to. Achebe must borrow Time from the new gods of Time to preserve the Time when the old god of Time ruled their Time. When Achebe is not at his desk, he has the wish to accelerate through the in-between parts of the business of life and the business of preserving Time. He longs for the impossible moments when in writing, he, Achebe becomes a minor god of Time. Achebe becomes the author of Time: of Simple Present, Past Perfect, Future Continuous; Past Continuous, Present Perfect, Simple Future; Simple Past, Present Perfect Continuous, Future Perfect. Achebe becomes a minor god, pausing and preserving Time: a god of a past, present, and future that can be revisited in a way that our Time can never be. Achebe becomes a minor god, with the ability to conjure more Time than any person could ever live as he conjures generations and lineages. Achebe becomes a minor god creating a new tempo for Time: granting a chapter to a day, while not even sparing a full sentence to a century. Achebe sits at his desk expending seconds hours days months years of his finite Time borrowed from the new gods so that he may write back to them and recover the dignity of the old gods of Time. How many others will make this trade of Time?

Time Passes

9 February 2016. Past midnight.

You are tired now, as are the other Comrades and Pinky. Down the corridor you hear someone whisper 'I have cigarettes,' to whoever might be listening. You ask Brenda for some of her snuff. The big sneeze, as always, leaves you somewhat comforted; you hug yourself and pull your knees to your stomach. You roll over, face the shit-streaked cinder block, try to sleep, shorten the ordeal. You hear the Comrades continue.

Time Passes

26 February 1946.

Malcolm Little at the beginning of his Time in Massachusetts state prisons. The beginning of six and a half years is the first time he has Time to be still. To reflect, to contemplate and cultivate the spirit that will transform Little to X. When will men like him get the time to be still?

Time Passes

12 January 2010.

An earthquake in Haiti. Swallows land, buildings, Fatiman's people. Almost as soon as the earth breaks, confusion, heartbreak, finger pointing spreads. The next day, US televangelist Robert Patson believes his god has given him the answer. Voodoo is not to blame. A sin greater than heathenism has been committed. You see, the devil has come back for Fatiman and Touissant's people, the only ones to have ever reclaimed their Time. But now we see that they had not truly succeeded after all. Their Time had been borrowed from the devil, returned now for his due. The people nod and cry. Indeed, the defeat was so singular across all of the Atlantic, it could not have been true. The people nod and cry, can any ever reclaim their Time?

Time Passes

Sometime. 9 February 2016.

'Afrika Bambaataa take the Hotep Cake spelling Africa with a k, naming themselves after a Zulu chief and Egyptian iconography for a crew logo!'

'How Sway?'

'I need answers!'

'You ain't got the answers!'

'Who wants to start the definitive list of Hotep's favourite tribal affiliations?'

'We can start with Nubia.'

'Then Zulu.'

'Then Xhosa–'

'—Not Tosa like KDot says?'

'You mean Kendrick when Xhosa and Zulu called the Crips and the Bloods?'

'My ancestors are wailing in underrepresentation!'

'Leave Kdot alone. He was inspired. He'd just come back from the Motherland!'

'He should have come to the Motherland to get inspired by me. I would've shown him his roots.'

'Hello Kunta Kinte.'

Time Passes

July 1898.

Salisbury jail. Rhodes' people did not know. Yes. Yes, some may say a medium is just an empty bag after the spirit leaves the body. During the first war against Rhodes' people, I possessed Charwe. I spoke out in my name, Nehanda Nyamhita Nyakasikana. After many battles in that war, Rhodes' people captured me.

They brought us here to Fort Salisbury prison, stood us against the wall and took pictures. 'Look, your great witch is just flesh and blood, which can be cut and spilled. Where is the spirit now?' They tried me, called me a witch. I danced, I sang, I screamed, I laughed, and told Rhodes' people the truth. 'You people may have won the first war, but you will not last, not even as long as the Portuguese!'

They sent that Richardtz to convert me. I danced, I sang, I screamed, I shouted and laughed at their Jesus. 'How can your god's son save me from this hell you speak of? How can your god's son promise life after death when our ancestors live among us now?' On that platform I shouted out that my bones would rise again.

Mapfupa achamuka!

I sang our freedom when they put the black bag over my head. I was still singing freedom when the rope broke my neck, and the song carried my spirit across time, returned me to the great waters of our ancestors again. Rhodes' people did not know. How could they?

Time Passes

1803.

Igbo people decide to end the fear of Time. The new gods of Time stole them from their land and packed them on a ship to the New World that makes slaves of the old gods. Resistance! The old gods of Time steal the ship. Landing on the shores of South Sea Islands of Georgia, the old gods cannot turn back. To do so will be to forever enslave their Time to the new gods. They look forward to how they might reclaim their Time. They look out onto the sea waves advancing and retreating on the shoreline; life, and death in rhythm like that, they see the world's indifference to the beginning or ending of life and weigh it against their concern. They look out onto the sea and imagine how they will claim their Time from the world's indifference. They look out onto the sea and imagine how they will make their Time surrender to them and them alone. They look at Death with clear eyes, confronting their Time's persistence with death's inevitability. The old gods look at Death, choose it, walk into the sea. Back to Africa, gods once more, no more fear of Time. Will we ever be so clear eyed?

Time Passes

Some Time.
  'Aluta continua Comrades.'
  'Me, I'm Tired.'
  'Umzabalazo this, Umzabalazo that.'
  'Prevailing.'
  'Overcoming.'
  'Fuck that shit.'

Time Passes

9 February 2016. Middle of the night.

'Abraham, against all hope, in hope I believed.'

'I bear all things, I believe all things, I have hope in all things, I endure all things.'

'Shem, when Paul wasn't being dogmatic and homophobic, he wrote nice things.'

'Talk to me about ancestors and I'll listen, none of this yt jesus shit.'

'I'm waiting for the day Mdalidiphu defeats Thixo.'

'Izwe.'

Time Passes

Some Time.
 'Black?'
 'Yes.'

Time Passes

Some Time.
'What I meant to say is that faith in Blackness is necessarily theological...At least for me anyway.'

Time Passes

Some Time.
 'Kana, what did Fela say?'
 'Who know no know go know.'

Time Passes

Some Time.

'Angazi, I don't have any big Hope. All I have is Small. Sometimes it's just singing with Comrades at Azania House, finishing a poem I've been working on for a while...or...Seven Colours on Sunday, Wilson B Nkosi blasting all day, my girl retwisting my locs, falling in and out of sleep in her lap...I don't know...no...Angazi, but I'm sure, if I didn't have those small graces, I'd go crazy.'

'Are you saying we're crazy Brenda?'

'Argh, Lumka, you know what I mean man... If I didn't have those things, I might just have decided to end it.'

Some Time.
　'Blackness is not here yet.'

Time Passes

Some Time.
　'Mayibuye iAfika?'
　'Silinde ukuza kuka Nxele.'

Time Passes

9 February 2016. 11:07.

You are all released, leaving Pinky behind in your shit-streaked holding cell. For two days, you hole yourself up in your room.

Time Passes

1819.

eRhini. The place known at this Moment in Time as grahamstown. uNxele, our prophet, sees into the Future the coming of the new gods of time. There they come! They have crossed iQagqiwa and they have crossed iNqweke, only one river more, iNxuba, and then they will be in our land. What will become of you then? uNxele leads His People in daytime attack against the new gods of Time, who, victorious, declare that history will not be on his side at that Moment in Time. The new gods sentence uNxele to Time, there he sits in his cell on the place known at this Moment in Time as robben island. Fed up, impatient uNxele and the frontier rebels escape! To the shoreline! The waters that brought the end of Our Time, treacherous once again, capsize their boats. Leading the rebels to shore, uNxele drowns. His People preserve his belongings, refusing to believe it, wait for His Return. Who knows where Our Time goes? For the answer to that I'm afraid we'll wait, silinde ukuza kukaNxele.

Time Passes

1873.

uNxele's People put away uNxele's belongings, resign themselves to Time no longer theirs. Who knows where Our Time goes? Someone asks. Silence answers. Buza uNxele, someone eventually suggests. We nod in agreement, uNxele is Our Prophet after all. Yes, we decide we will wait for uNxele. Silinde ukuza kukaNxele. But we don't know if this waiting is our maturity or cowardice, or the maturity of cowardice, or the cowardice of maturity? Perhaps if the prophet returned to answer he would say, Our Time is swallowed up in the Black holes of the universe which continually expands with its propensity to steal Our Time. They learn to shrug their shoulders and say, Who knows where Our Time goes? For the answer to that I'm afraid we'll wait, silinde ukuza kukaNxele.

Time Has Passed

Some Time.

Ukuza KukaNxele. Maybe that day, if uNxele, our prophet after all, knows where Our Time goes, he will tell us when He Returns. If uNxele, our prophet after all, knows where Our Time goes, does he know how we can get it back, earn it back, buy it back, claim it back, make it Black? All the Time that's gone by? Who knows where Our Time goes? For the answer to that I'm afraid we'll wait, silinde ukuza kukaNxele.

WTF are commons?

Mithu Sanyal

Translated from German by Lucy Jones

> '*The law locks up the man or woman*
> *Who steals the goose from off the common*
> *But leaves the greater villain loose*
> *Who steals the common from off the goose.*'
> (English protest song, circa 17th century)

The first time I heard about commons was in Great Britain. And 'heard' is the operative word because commons is the name given to all kinds of places – Clapham Common, Wimbledon Common, Mungrisdale Common, Hay Common – and it always refers to land that is no longer common. Let me explain!

The concept of commons has existed since time immemorial – which in England means since 1086[4]. It refers to land that belonged to the

---

4 In 1086, on the orders of King William the First, better known as William the Conqueror, a land survey was drawn up listing all the king's subjects and their taxable value – i.e. houses and land – and recorded in the Domesday Book.

people, on which they had permission to plant their vegetables, graze their livestock, gather firewood and cut peat. Commons are recorded as far back as the Domesday Book. But at the end of the 12th century, the Enclosures Movement began, which led to common land being fenced off and privatised by lords and major landowners. (This begs the question of how they became major landowners in the first place.)

What started slowly at first, soon picked up speed. At the beginning of industrialisation, land was no longer land but capital that could be calculated in concrete terms: If I have *this* many sheep, this means that in half a year I will have *this* many sacks of wool. Sheep, therefore, were more profitable than commoners. To give the process a semblance of legality, Parliament passed a flurry of Enclosure Acts – in 1773, 1845, 1846, 1847, 1848, 1849, 1851, 1852, 1854, 1857, 1859, 1868, 1876, 1878, 1879 and 1882 – against which an even greater number of commoners fought.

I've often wondered why the big interest groups for social equality in the (Dis-) United Kingdom had such evocative names, such as the Levellers and Diggers movement. The answer is that the Levellers tore down fences and filled in (or 'levelled') ditches that cut off access to the commons; the Diggers, on the other hand,

---

That is why in England the phrase 'since time immemorial' means since 1086.

continued to farm (or 'dig') illegally on the commons, even though the landowners sent armed gangs to stop them or, failing that, the army – which resulted in more riots and harder crackdowns by the government, and so on.

The Enclosure Riots were the biggest social protests of the 16th and 17th centuries. After all, an entire way of life was at stake. Karl Marx called the Enclosures Movement and the violent destruction of the commons economy the precursor of capitalism because it uprooted a class of people who could then not lead subsistent lives, and were therefore forced to sell their labour on the market. By the mid-19th century, what remained of the commons were mostly place names, in which the sorrow of the enclosures echoed down the generations.

I was horrified when I found this out. It hadn't always been the case that we'd had no right to the land we live on? Why didn't I know that? The second shock was when I realised that in Germany there used to be commons too, of course! What had I thought the Peasants' Wars had been about? Only in Germany, commons were called *Allmenden* (from the Middle High German *Allgemeinde*) and have been so effectively erased from the collective consciousness that most of us don't even know their name. Well, that's not entirely fair: in the Alps, parts of Bavaria, and Switzerland, *Allmenden* do still exist. But it shows how removed people are from this tradition that, like in so many other areas of knowledge production, we resort to a vocabulary and theories taken from England and the US with the consequence that here, too, we don't speak of *Allmenden* but of *commons*.

But, to return to my first shock. The idea that public space, as well as the water we drink and the air we breathe, belongs to us all, turned my worldview upside down. Why had I accepted the exact opposite until now? Even though I have been fighting the effects of this alienation for as long as I can remember. I don't mean fighting in the sense that the Levellers and Diggers fought – by putting their lives on the line – but rather the way people fight, by writing a strongly worded letter to their newspaper or texts like this. My first protest was in the 1980s when the German National Garden Show was going to take place in my hometown of Düsseldorf and the city planners decided to transform the Volksgarten park into one enormous Südpark. Our protest group was made up of allotment gardeners whose land would be taken away by the development, neighbours who were appalled by the proposal to fence off a public park and charge admission, and teenagers like myself who objected to the park's future night-time closure because that's where we made out with our girl or boyfriends. In our petition, we explained how hard the consequences of these measures would hit our community. But it did not occur to us to fundamentally question the city's right to take away *our* park just like that, no questions asked – Volksgarten translates as 'The People's Park', the clue is in the name!

The Volksgarten was created in 1893 because the workers who slaved away in the steelworks in Oberbilk, the poorest part of Düsseldorf, had been dropping like flies. So the city decided – no, not to build a functioning sewer system or more housing – but to build a park instead, and in doing so, the life expectancy of the Oberbilk district inhabitants significantly increased in one fell swoop. Air pollution and working conditions were still spectacularly bad, but the basic fact that people could see trees and flowers and sit on some grass made an enormous difference. Okay, later the city did install showers so that people could wash, and even later, a hospital was set up. But common land, even if people are not allowed to plant vegetables on it, has a value that should not be underestimated.

The oldest plant found to date on a human settlement is 23,000 years old. It's a flower that looks like a small, yellow daisy. You can't eat it and it doesn't have any medicinal properties, but it still grew in abundance by the Sea of Galilee. Why? Probably because people liked it. Beauty does something to our psyche, but also our immune system. People who live in cities with very little green around them are more likely to develop cardiovascular problems – but that has nothing to do with environmental pollution. Lack of nature seems to be enough to make people ill. Also, parks and communal gardens are not just precious to our health; they reduce criminality, too, and much more effectively than CCTV cameras. But there is a caveat: this only works where gardens are not surrounded by insurmountable fences. If they are, people tend to throw their rubbish over those fences, probably as a reaction to feeling locked out. If, on the other hand, gardens are only surrounded by walls low enough to sit on, they turn into social meeting places and strengthen the feelings of responsibility that people have towards them. This doesn't just apply to urban crime hotspots but also global ones. For example, the Lemon Tree Trust, which helps build gardens in refugee camps, was surprised that 70 per cent of the plants that people decided to grow were flowers, although they desperately needed vegetables. That's because beauty is just as important for our survival as nutrition. As the writer George Sand insisted: 'organise luxury for all…since you do not have schools, open free gardens and theatres, give free concerts and festivals, establish free museums.'[5]

Luckily, back in the 80s, we didn't manage to stop the German National Garden Show, which

---

5   George Sand, 'Reverie à Paris', originally published in 1867 as 'Luxury for All', translated and with an introduction by Gideon Fink Shapiro, in: *Places Journal*, January 2022.

had been one of our demands. What we *did* manage to prevent was the lovely extended park being enclosed and fenced off. This meant that the Volksgarten was still the neighbourhood lifeline and remained literally the park of the people: they drank tea from samovars on its meadows, had barbecues, and handed out food to passers-by. In the Volksgarten, no one asks whether they're allowed to walk on the grass. Everyone is permitted to be here. That's especially important because, for many who live in Oberbilk, this is only true to a limited extent. It's an area of town where racial profiling – in other words, stopping and searching people without due reason – is legal. The police term for these kinds of places is *disreputable and dangerous areas*. The dangerous part being that the majority of people who live there come from immigrant backgrounds, which is why racial profiling ... – a circular argument confirming that public space is not common ground at all.

I agree with Marx that the Enclosures should go down in the history books as one of the greatest crimes against humanity. Instead, we read that the Enclosures were necessary to make agriculture more effective and to feed the growing population. With what? Sheep's wool? Which lords opened soup kitchens and distributed bread and roses to the people?

What's almost more cynical – although they are neck and neck in the race – is the theory by the ecologist Garrett Hardin, who published an influential article in 1968 with the title '*The Tragedy of the Commons*'[6], which he based on the pamphlet of the same name by economist William Forster Lloyd from 1833. Hardin explained that the commons, which had functioned well for centuries (and probably millennia), were doomed to failure. Like Lloyd before him, he uses the example of a hypothetical pasture on which every villager keeps ten sheep. Hardin concludes that each person would try to add an 11th sheep – and then another and another – because this would maximise his or her profit. But the costs (for example, less pasture for the herd) would be shared by everyone until that common would inevitably be overgrazed – and there you have the tragedy of the commons. Apart from the fact that commoners were able to talk to each other and make agreements for the good of everyone and the pasture, what's most interesting about this view is how it depicts humans as blindly self-interested beings who require an overpowering leviathan of a state to force them not to hit each other over the head all the time.

We have a similarly fatalistic worldview when it comes to nature. Robin Wall Kimmerer is professor for Environmental Studies and a First Nation American; she is a member of the Citizen Potawatomi Nation. At the beginning of

---

6   Garrett Hardin, 'The Tragedy of the Commons', in: *Science*, New Series, Vol. 162, Issue 3859, December 1968.

an environmental-based programme, Kimmerer gave her students a survey in which they had to rate their understanding of the interactions between humans and the environment. All 200 students claimed that humans were harmful to the environment: that they were destructive, exploitative, the instigators of climate change and that they contaminated fields and polluted water – we know the list. Later in the survey, they were asked whether they knew of any positive interactions between humans and the environment. The answer was: no. Kimmerer was appalled that her students could not even *imagine* what a positive interaction might look like, especially as these were young people who had chosen this study programme because they wanted to protect the environment. But like all of us, they had grown up with the narrative that we are separated from each other and the world around us, individuals on a speck of dust hurtling through space. But if we perceive ourselves as separate from nature, we can't interact with it meaningfully. All we can do is exploit the environment or save it, but not live with and from each other on an equal footing.

An example of how this might be done is 'the honourable harvest' which is Kimmerer's term for the traditional handling of gifts of nature: never pick the first berry you find so that you'll never pick the last, give something back to the plant to express gratitude, such as a song or a prayer, scattering seeds, and so on. To test the effectiveness of the honourable harvest scientifically, Kimmerer introduced an experiment at her university. On a meadow, a PhD student planted plots of sweetgrass, which is threatened with extinction in the USA. She left a section of the plots completely untouched, which roughly corresponds to our idea of conservation: pick nothing. She harvested one section by carefully cutting the stalks – but only half of them. And in the third section, she ripped out the grasses, the way basket weavers traditionally do, by pulling the roots out of the ground – but also only half the stalks.

The biggest challenge for the PhD student was to express her gratitude for the gift of the sweetgrass. Yet over the months, she developed a personal connection to the grass, even if she could not bring herself to sing to it. The result of the experiment was that the sweetgrass on the plots that had been left fallow was interspersed with dead stalks at the end of the observation period of two years, while it thrived and multiplied on the plots that had been harvested. And this foremost in the sections where the grasses had been ripped out (take note, this only works with sweetgrass!) [7] Humans are not the parasites of the planet. We have something to give! But to

---

[7] Cf. Robin Wall Kimmerer, *Braiding Sweetgrass*. Minneapolis, 2015; Chapter: 'The Honorable Harvest'

do this, we need to access the knowledge and practices on how this can be done.

The Enclosures did not just convert human beings into a labour force but also changed nature from an entity with which we lived in an intimate relationship – because we were de facto related – to a resource to be exploited. If we no longer see a tree as a subject with which we interact but as an object that we can saw into planks, we create a barrier between the tree and us. We have no moral responsibility towards the tree anymore. In this way, we not only cut off our compassion for the tree but also ourselves from the living world around us.

That's why it was such a victory for activists in New Zealand in 2017 when the Whanganui River was recognised as a legal person – a goal they had been fighting to achieve for 140 years. 'The reason we have taken this approach is that we consider the river an ancestor and always have,' said Gerrard Albert, the lead negotiator for the Whanganui iwi [tribe].[8] The news circulated through the media as a curiosity, as something peculiar to the Māori, that had precious little to do with the rest of us. Yet people all over the world campaign for the rights of rivers, lakes, mountains, forests, moors and so on, to be recognised as persons by law.

---

8   Quoted from Eleanor Aigne Roy, 'New Zealand river granted same legal rights as human being', in: *The Guardian*, (16.03.2017).

At the same time as the Whanganui River in New Zealand, for example, the Yamuna River and the Ganges in India were recognised as living entities. A few months later, however, the Supreme Court of India overturned the ruling because that would have made it possible to sue the industries that pollute them. Since then, it has been unclear what the hell the Yamuna and Ganges are supposed to be – only legally of course. For those who immerse themselves into these waters to pay their respects, they have always been living entities. These interventions are not only about prevention but also and above all about the need to enter into meaningful relationships with more-than-human entities.

For the same reason, the performance artists and sex ecologists Annie Sprinkle and Beth Stephens make a case for changing the paradigm 'from Earth as mother to Earth as lover.'[9] In other words, let's stop just demanding sustenance and resources from nature and enter into a reciprocal relationship instead. In their workshops, Sprinkle and Stephen teach the practices of protest, but also how to ask trees for consent before hugging them. This sounds very hippyish – until you take part in one of their workshops and then it seems like the most natural thing in the world.

---

9 Cf. Annie Sprinkle und Beth Stephens with Jenny Klein, *Assuming the Ecosexual Position. The Earth as Lover*. Minneapolis 2021.

And then came the Coronavirus crisis and the Icelandic government advised its citizens to 'hug a tree' if they felt desperate.[10]

So that's exactly what I did: I went into the Volksgarten and hugged trees. It was one of the most effective interventions against the feeling of being closed off from a public space which had become hostile to me. It helped that at the beginning of 2020, the Volksgarten was one of the few places that wasn't cordoned off with red-and-white police tape. An hour in the park was an hour of mental and emotional health.

On their website, the Icelandic government explained that hugging trees helped overcome loneliness and isolation. True, if I'm not allowed to hug anything or anyone else, I can at least hug a tree. But this interspecies intimacy is more than just a substitution. Studies show that people who are connected to nature are less prone to depression because they feel connected to the world. On a similar note, the clinical psychiatrist Sue Stuart-Smith shows in her book *The Well Gardened Mind*[11] that convalescence in hospitals is significantly accelerated if patients can see a tree from their window, rather than just other hospital buildings – and it is even quicker if they

---

10 Cf. 'Icelanders urged to hug trees to overcome isolation', in: *BBC News* (25.04.2020).
11 Sue Stuart-Smith, *The Well Gardened Mind: Rediscovering Nature in the Modern World*, London 2020.

are taken into one of the rare hospital gardens. This is extremely relevant research considering that visitors in Great Britain are not even allowed to bring flowers into hospitals for health and safety reasons.

Nature is not just outside; it is the extension of our mental and emotional space. It is what the author Ian Sinclair, and before him Guy Debord and the Situationists, called 'psychogeography'. For this reason, anthropologist Neera Singh researched the affective and emotional impact of the commons using the example of community-based forests in Odisha, India. Obviously, the British predator class not only enclosed common land at home but also – and much more radically – in their colonies. In Odisha, for example, most of the forests were enclosed and used (read: exploited) for intensive timber extraction. This practice continued in postcolonial India until the forests were threatened with extinction and villagers began to dig up the roots of the trees to make fires and cook food. For this reason, in the 1990s, numerous villages formed communities to protect the forests. Now more than 10,000 villages in Odisha are part of the Community Forests Agreement.

'One village leader simply described the collective action to protect forests as 'Samaste samaste ko bandhi ke achanti', that is, 'each and every 'one' holds the other together.' I think he was also referring to the affective capacities of all bodies, human and nonhuman, to come together and get entangled in relations of affect and accountability',[12] Singh explains.

Commoning – because commons are not a thing but an action and therefore a verb[13] – is always an expression of compassion, coexistence and love. As early as 2007, the political scientist Elinor Ostrom expanded the concept of the commons to include knowledge as a shared resource. And this immaterial common ground – such as knowledge, time, codes and the genome – is equally threatened at the moment by corresponding immaterial enclosures. Companies and corporations are itching to patent the genetic codes of (medicinal) plants and even human beings. Besides this, the new digital commons, such as open-source software and so on, present their own challenges. For example, Wikipedia is the dream of a knowledge resource that is not only shared but also democratically created – and yet 90 per cent of the authors are male, 85 per cent have a university education and 81 per cent are from the global North.

---

12 Singh, N.M.: 'The affective labor of growing forests and the becoming of environmental subjects: Rethinking environmentality in Odisha, India', *Geoforum* (2013), http://dx.doi.org/10.1016/j.geoforum.2013.01.010
13 The use of 'commoning' as a verb was popularised by the historian Peter Linnebaugh.

However, with these new challenges, a revival of the commons is also taking place. The term *common ground* now refers to a communication model that participants use to communicate with one another to reach a common goal – in other words, to understand others and be understood. The discourse, therefore, becomes a collective act that leads to new common knowledge, making commoning a new form of cooperation beyond the market and the state. The economist and historian Friederike Habermann calls it the 'ecommony'. Sociologist Simon Sutterlütti and computer scientist Stefan Meretz from the Commons Institute go one step further and talk about 'commonism'.

'Revival of the commons, then,' Singh finishes, 'becomes critical not simply from the perspective of restoration of access and control over physical resources, but from the perspective of countering this alienation and finding a way to produce alternate subjectivities and alternate worlds. From this perspective, we need to reclaim the commons as material resources not only for subsistence and livelihood but also as the grounds for the production of subjectivity.'[14]

---

14 Neera Singh: 'Becoming a commoner: The commons as sites for affective socio-nature encounters and co-becomings' In: www.ephemerajournal.org, Vol. 17(4), 2017, p. 762.

Authors

Azhari Aiyub was born in Banda Aceh (1981). He was awarded first prize in the Ministry of Education and Culture's short story writing competition in 2003, before receiving the Poets of All Nations' Free Word Award in 2005. In 2007 he received fellowship from the International Institute for Asian Studies (IIAS) in Amsterdam and Leiden. In 2015 Azhari was selected for a writer's residency in Mexico, resulted in his travelogue *Tembok, Polanco, dan Alien: Suatu Petualangan Kecil ke Negeri Meksiko* [*Wall, Polanco and Alien: A Little Adventure in Mexico*] (2019). His short story collections *Perempuan Pala* [*Nutmeg Woman*] and *The Garden of Delights & Other Tales* have been translated into English, German and French. His almost 1,000 pages novel, *Kura-kura Berjanggut* [*The Bearded Turtle*] won 2018 Khatulistiwa Literary Award.

Yásnaya Elena Aguilar Gil (Ayutla Mixe, 1981) is an ayuujk linguist, writer, translator, linguistic rights activist and researcher. She is part of Colegio Mixe, a collective organization that aims to disseminate their research on Mixe language, history and culture. Some of her texts have been published in the anthologies *Condolerse* (Sur+, 2015), *El futuro es hoy. Ideas radicales para México* (Biblioteca Nueva, 2018), *Tsunami* (Sexto Piso, 2018) y *Un Nosotrxs sin Estado* (OnA ediciones, 2018), among others. In 2020 *Ää: manifiestos sobre la diversidad*

lingüística, an anthology of essays on linguistic diversity, was published by Almadia. She has participated in several projects related to spreading knowledge about linguistic diversity, development of grammar content for textbooks and didactic material on indigenous languages and documentation projects on languages on the brink of extinction.

Uxue Alberdi Estibaritz is an author and *bertsolari* (Basque folk singer) born in Elgoibar, 1984. She writes short stories, novels, essays, historic literature, and children's literature. She has received the Basque Literature Award on two occasions, once for her children's book *Besarkada ('Hug')*, and again for her essay *Kontrako Eztarritik* ('Down the wrong chute'). Her most recent novel, *Jenisjoplin*, was awarded the *111 Akademia* prize, and translated into Spanish and English.

Panashe Chigumadzi is an essayist and novelist. Chigumadzi is the author of *These Bones Will Rise Again* (2018), which was shortlisted for the 2019 Alan Paton Prize for Non-fiction. Her debut novel *Sweet Medicine*, won the 2016 K. Sello Duiker Literary Award. Chigumadzi was the founding editor of Vanguard Magazine, a platform for black women coming of age in post-apartheid South Africa.

Authors

Cristina Judar was born in São Paulo, is a writer and journalist, author of the novel 'The women who marched under the sun' (2021), just sold to Arabic and Mozambique, and 'Oito do sete', winner of Prêmio São Paulo de Literatura 2018 and shortlisted for Prêmio Jabuti 2018. She is also the author of 'Roteiros de uma vida curta', the graphic novels 'Lina' and 'Vermelho, vivo' and the art project 'Questions for a live writing' conceived during an artist residency at Queen Mary University of London. Her short stories were translated and published in literary supplements and anthologies in the US, UK and Egypt (she is in this very recently published anthology organized in the US).

Nesrine Khoury was born in Syria in 1983 and lives in Alicante, Spain. Her first book of poetry, 'With a Drag of War', was published in 2015 by Attakwin, Damascus. Her novel, 'Wadi Qandil', was published by Al-Mutawassit in 2017. She is translated into English, Spanish, French, Catalan and Italian.

Mithu Sanyal is an author, a cultural scientist and a journalist. She published a cultural history of the *Vulva* (Wagenbach; *Vulva: A Revelation of the Invisible Sex*, 2009) and one of rape (*Vergewaltigung. Aspekte eines Verbrechens*, 2016, Nautilus; English translation *Rape. From Lucretia to #MeToo*, 2019). Her debut novel *Identitti* (2021, Hanser) was awarded the Ernst-Bloch-Preis and the regional literature award Literaturpreis Ruhr, and it was shortlisted for the German Book Prize.

Translators

Mikael Johani is a poet and translator in Jakarta. His poetry veers between flarfy broken l=a=n=g=u=a=g=e games and thin descriptions of les petites histoires d'indonésie. His works have appeared in Poems by Sunday, The Book of Jakarta, #UntitledThree, On Relationships, Asymptote, The Johannesburg Review of Books, AJAR, Vice Indonesia, Kerja Tangan, and Popteori. He is the author of the poetry collection *We Are Nowhere And It's Wow* (Post Press, 2017). He organises Paviliun Puisi, a monthly spoken word night in Jakarta.

Lucy Jones lives in Berlin, where she co-founded Transfiction, a translators' collective, and runs the Fiction Canteen reading series. She has translated works by Anke Stelling, Theresia Enzensberger and Brigitte Reimann, among others, for Penguin, Scribe and Dialogue Books. Her own writing has been published in Litro Magazine, SAND Journal, Visual Verse, Pigeon Papers NY and 3AM Magazine.

Joshua Rackstraw is a writer, teacher and translator from Manchester, currently based in Bilbao, Spain. His first book, *Malas Decisiones*, was published in 2020. His interests include art, technology, ethics, and Basque and Spanish culture. He was the official translator of the Zaragoza Declaration, a text on AI ethics co-funded by the Creative Europe Programme of the European Union.

Julia Sanches translates books from Portuguese, Spanish, and Catalan into English. Born in Brazil, she lives in the Northeast of the United States.

Jonathan Wright is a translator and former Reuters journalist. His previous translations from the Arabic include Khaled Al Khamissi's *Taxi*, Youssef Ziedan's *Azazeel* (Winner of the IPAF, 2009), Saud Alsanousi's *The Bamboo Stalk* (Winner of the IPAF, 2013), Hammour Ziada's *The Longing of the Dervish* (Winner of the Naguib Mahfouz Prize), Ahmed Saadawi's *Frankenstein in Baghdad* (shortlisted for the Man Booker International), Mazen Maarouf's *Jokes for the Gunmen* (shortlisted for the Man Booker International), and Hassan Blasim's *God 99*, *The Madman of Freedom Square* and *The Iraqi Christ* (winner of the 2014 Independent Foreign Fiction Prize).

Publishers

Almadía is a Mexican publishing house that publishes narratives, essays, and poetry. It was founded in 2005 in Oaxaca, a territory in the south of the country that is characterized by its linguistic and cultural diversity. In our catalogue, we have sought to echo this origin through books that help us to capture the wealth and complexity of the world we inhabit.

Founded in 2015 in Milan, **Al-Mutawassit** is focused on Arabic classical and contemporary literature and poetry, as well as international literature in Arabic translation. It has published authors like Giuseppe Tomasi di Lampedusa, Paul Auster, Javier Marías, Joyce Carol Oates, Dunya Mikhail, Mazen Maarouf and Hassan Blasim.

consonni is a publisher based in an independent cultural space located in the San Francisco district of Bilbao. Since 1996 we have been producing critical culture and at present we have opted for the printed word – together with the word that is whispered, heard, silenced or recited. From the expanded field of art, literature, the radio and education, our ambition is to alter the world that we inhabit and in turn to be altered by it.

Dublinense is an independent publishing house created in 2009 in Porto Alegre, southern Brazil. It was born with the free spirit and openness to experiment through different genres and styles. Through the journey, Dublinense found its true nature publishing literary fiction and non-fiction. It looks for literature capable of leading conversations about important subjects both from voices from different cultures abroad and the new Brazilian literary scene, chasing for good, fun, exciting and relevant books.

HATJE CANTZ Hatje Cantz is an international publisher who specializes in art, architecture, photography, design, culture and lifestyle. Since 1945, Hatje Cantz has been producing and publishing illustrated books with special demands on quality and content. Since 2019, the Berlin-based publisher has opened up its program in various ways: The Hatje Cantz Text series is dedicated to contemporary discourses on art and publishes texts by artists, curators, and many voices from different practices. Since summer 2021, the portfolio has been extended to include a children's art book program.

MARJIN KIRI Founded in Tangerang Selatan, Indonesia, in 2005, **Marjin Kiri** is a left wing publisher with focus on humanities, social sciences, Marxist literature, progressive politics and literature.

txalaparta Txalaparta (Navarra, Spain) has been publishing books in Basque and Spanish for over 30 years. An independent, left-wing, publishing house; it is dedicated to historical memory and critical thought. It publishes narratives and essays from national and international authors, for both adults and children, always maintaining the highest standards of literary quality. Work is carried out collectively (in *Auzolan*), as it is the most enriching way to work.